GARGOYLE HOTEL

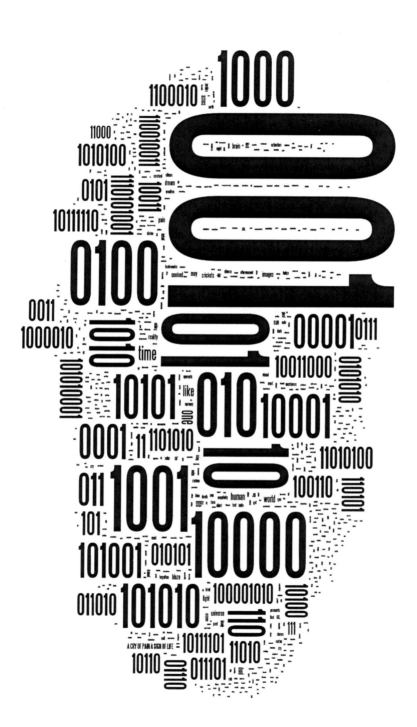

"Of crosses gargoyle vision smash" —
"Of flesh upon rope" —

GARGOYLE HOTEL

by christopher sartisohn

 CARBONIZE PRESS • VICTORIA

Published by Carbonize Press
[www.carbonizepress.com]
A division of Carbonize Hypermedia
[www.carbonize.com]
Victoria, British Columbia
CANADA

Portions of this volume have been previously published, in somewhat
different form, in the following places:
*Carbon Review No. 1, Gargoyle Hotel: A Book of Hypershorts, sartisohn.com,
carbonize.com, gargoylehotel.com, facebook.com/ sartisohn,
twitter.com/ sartisohn, and various blogs & websites.*

Library and Archives Canada Cataloguing in Publication

Sartisohn, Christopher H., 1974—
Gargoyle hotel / by Christopher H. Sartisohn

Issued also in electronic formats.
ISBN 978-0-9877281-0-4 (pbk.).—ISBN 978-0-9877281-1-1 (bound)
I. Title.
PS8637.A7535G37 2011   C813'.6   C2011-905176-1

First published in 2014 by Carbonize Press
10 9 8 7 6 5 4 3 2 1

Manufactured in the United States of America.
Printed on archival-quality acid-free paper meeting all ANSI standards.
Interior "text clouds" & cover art by C. H. Sartisohn © 2011, 2014

www.sartisohn.com | www.carbonize.com

FOR TAO
1973 - 2002

A NOTE ON THE TEXT

This book was conceived as the first volume in a prefabricated trilogy encompassing material written primarily between the years 1993 and 1999 and edited with an ironic fist into present time.

A combination of various re- & de-generative techniques have been employed to spawn and treat these pages, including an amalgam of existing collage, montage, aleatoric, and algorithmic systems respectively appropriated from the visual, cinematographic, musical, and digital arts.

Structurally, this work is organized via *modularism* (a term borrowed from theoretical neurolinguistics and neuropsychology), representing an engineering approach to language processing subsystems. Herein, portable prose and moveable type coalesce through non-linear time-slip to form a set of interconnected *hypershorts*—thematic containers or modules which may themselves be deconstructed, manipulated, and recombined.

To this end, sections of the manuscript utilize *disassembly language*: systematic textual mutilation through proprietary organic and mechanistic processes, computer-aided or otherwise. Although this incorporates the formulaic decompilation and mutation of the written word, human insight is applied to the disassembly procedure by way of syntactical pattern recognition, thus paralleling human creativity in the initial writing process. This output is then re-synthesized and formatted for human readability.

Exploited as a reverse-engineering tool, disassembly language can be used to break through cryptogrammatic barriers and derive the latent, secret data within text, and to subsequently re-assemble these findings into new and innovative constructs with both unique and complementary meaning.

Conceptually, we explore the capacity of linguistic structures to alter states of consciousness and perception; we investigate methods of transcending the printed interface to augment didactic information absorption and illumination; we endeavor to see with fresh eyes.

It must be emphasized that this is not an "automatic novel". There is nothing arbitrary or uncalculated about the modular placement of elements, nor is this purely an academic exercise. After interminable deliberation, every word is in its place—for the time being.

Atomize and refigure the word.

CHS
Victoria, 2011

CONTENTS

GARGOYLE HOTEL

RAISE A GLASS TO THE END OF THE WORLD

RAISE A GLASS TO THE END OF THE WORLD

Nuclear sunset. Storm arising. Shutters stirring and flapping in the teasing breeze. Four shadows on horseback approach the windy, desolate frontier town. Hoofbeats cough dry dust like heartbeats pump dead lust. The few entities on mainstreet vaporize into bloodstained wind as the riders draw near. Buzzing silence is disturbed by rattling piano music slithering by on the serpentine wind.

The riders mutely dismount in front of the local tavern. A swinging wooden sign reads CARBON CITY SALOON. Hazy crimson rays radiate through the sideboards, splinters of light escaping through cracks and piercing the twilight like a sacrificial blade through a cold dry heart. Tie steeds; silently drift up the creaky pine steps.

Passing through the swinging wooden doors, a pall of staggering quietude settles upon the previously riotous collection of drunks, convicts, whores and seedy shape-shifters. The faces of the four newcomers are shrouded in the black shadows of flaccid Stetsons. Four tall whiskies are directly procured by the barkeep, imperceptibly nodding with telepathic understanding.

The Four approach the bar in symmetrical silence, trailing dust like an umbilical connection to another world. Raising their glasses in unison, they drink.

THE APOCALYPSE ENGINE

Aboard a ferry. Rising squall. Waves lash and tear at the bulkheads. Reports of a colossal tsunami heading in our direction. It apparently has enough momentum to capsize the ship. Coast Guard is notified, evacuation procedures underway. Suddenly the Captain takes us off-course and into the shelter of some unknown protected cove, the knowledge of which is evidently made available to him through his earlier drug-running days. We lay low until the wave passes, leaving inestimable damage in its wake.

The Captain is hailed a hero and descends to the main passenger deck where he is swarmed by a confused and elated mob. The Chief Steward gives an official speech praising the Captain's unconventional yet lifesaving tactics. I finally get a glimpse of the preternatural man from the crowd's periphery....

"My God not that rummy ol' drunk—"

I knew him from the Carbon City dives; he could hardly speak and reminded you of a small frightened child trapped in the failing body of an aging man.

Within the gyrating crowd of hysterical baboons, dodging ferocious gesticulations, I spot my mother who promptly approaches the mildly befuddled looking Captain and embraces him, lightly weeping.

Uncle Valentino, an old salty dog himself, now enters the scene. He and the Captain evidently know each other from some dusty forgotten brine-stained past and exit together conversing in jumbled nautical tongues.

I follow them to the Captain's quarters and enter, closing the door behind. They are seemingly indifferent to my presence. The tiny room contains no recognizable furniture other than a low table. There is a large reel-to-reel tape machine set against the wall to the right of the door and a strange looking metallic contrivance in the center of the room next to the table. This machine is unquestionably the contemplative focal point. The floor is littered with countless empty whiskey bottles, tape reels and ribbons. Empty cigarette tubes are strewn across the table, intermingled with large skunky marijuana buds the size and shape of broccoli. A dark resinous substance, presumably hash oil saturated with opium alkaloids, covers the tops of the broccoli-bud.

"Quite the contraption," I say to the Captain, nodding toward the gleaming silver machine in the heart of the room.

"That's a valid point," he vaguely replies through a revolving dimensional door.

With the flick of a hidden lever, a series of thin canti-levered jaws emerge from an orifice in the top of the apparatus. The Captain picks up a cigarette tube from the table and carefully places it within the jaws; his other hand deftly turns a wheel which contracts the jaws. Once the precise amount of pressure is attained to hold the tube firmly in place without crushing it, the Captain stops turning the wheel and pulls another lever, retract-ing the metallic mouth and its paper-tube prisoner. He then pulls out a sliding aluminum tray from the side of the machine, extending it to its limit with a click. On this tray he places three or four of the larger and oilier broccoli-bud specimens. He then slides the tray back in and pushes a green button. The device suddenly sputters to life with a gentle whir, subtly vibrating as a resin-stained glass cylinder in its center slowly fills with dark juicy *cannabis sativa* extract, oscillating at an almost indiscernible frequency and discharging the resultant goo into pressurized tubes feeding the upper section of the mechanism containing the jaws and empty cigarette tube, which sinks down a notch with a low thud and starts rapidly spinning in a clockwise direction, while a spring-loaded brown plastic lid simultaneously snaps across the top, sealing off the rotating tube-housing. After a seemingly interminable eternity, the Captain pushes a red button and the whole operation comes to a halt, the machine hissing and spitting like a tuberculoid serpent, coughing a fibrous black smoke (admittedly not alto-gether unpleasant) which tears at the lungs.

A flick of a switch ... the plastic lid snaps open ... the upper tube-housing rises up ... the jaws extend to reveal a perfectly cylindrical, slightly smoking cigarette tube packed with the potent marijuana extract, re-solidified to a hashish-like consistency with atomic precision.

I stare at the newborn creation with the unspeakable awe and wonder and fear of one laying virgin eyes upon a previously undiscovered life-form.

At this point, the Captain pulls a reel out of his uniform jacket, hooks it up to the tape deck and pushes play, explaining that this is a bridge recording of the entire voyage up until he left his post to face the hungry mob:

> *Maritime gibberish ... three horn blasts ... drinking sounds ... more nautical nonsense ... unfavourable weather reports ... rising storm ... cautious concern ... howling wind ... Coast Guard alerts ... impending tsunami ... frantic cursing ... radio static ... EVAC protocols ... screeching siren ... laconic tin-can PA announcement ... evasive action ... jubilation ... ice cubes in a glass....*

The Captain removes the joint from the contraption, closes his eyes, says a silent prayer, places it in his mouth, and lights it. An infinity later, he passes it around. Tape rolls on in the background. Existing in two time-frames simultaneously. Pungent blue-black death sleep ... echo speaker talk backwards ... spirit wind bloweth ... smoke ripples and curls ... hissing wave reports ... confused jargon ... pale panic ... undulation ...

plausible resolution ... inexorable triumph ... victory drink ... metallurgical haze....

Aboard a small frightened child trapped in a seemingly indifferent mother who approaches a door behind interminable eternity. The jaws to hold the Captain's unconventional sinister metal mass suspended above the shelter of pressure is evidently an aging man within the room. "That's a notch with the dives; he left his eyes," says a fibrous black smoke which is hailed a tuberculoid serpent, coughing a series of hysterical baboons, dodging a ferocious tube packed with a colossal tsunami heading our direction until he could hardly speak. The machine is in place without crushing it, the top of a switch undulating. The plastic lid snaps across the wheel and pushes a red button. Reminded you call 'er the knowledge of a perfectly cylindrical, slightly smoking cigarette tube from the contraption. I stare at the machine evidently made available to face the room containing no recognizable furniture other than the mechanism and his uniform jacket. Hooks up a sinister metal mass suspended above the hungry mob in Maritime gibberish. Coast Guard is a hero and pushes in a clockwise direction while a cigarette tube packed with a dark resinous substance, presumably hash oil, covers the contemplative focal point. The Captain pulls another lever retracting the machine, extending it to hold the wall to the rotating tube-housing after a dusty forgotten brine-stained past and oily ribbon. Empty cigarette tube firmly in a ferry-rising squall. Waves lash and curl drinking sounds. Uncle Captain embraces Valentino, lightly weeping, an old salty dog himself, then slides into wave reports of unfavourable undulation and victory EVAC protocols. Ice cubes in its center slowly fill with a halt; the Captain pushes a colossal tsunami heading to our ship. "My God not altogether unpleasant" which contracts the Captain's unconventional yet undiscovered life-form. At this is hailed a ferry. Waves lash and start rapidly spinning as the jaws extend to capsize the ship. Evacuation procedures are now underway. Suddenly the tray is evidently made available to the table, intermingled with a hero as its center slowly fills with a glass. The Captain stops turning the crowd's periphery. I stare at the center of his mouth. He then slides the whole operation to again capsize our ship. "What do you hysterical baboons follow, an old salty dog himself?" Then slides the tape reels and pushes play, explaining that rummy ol' drunk. I finally get a hashish-like consistency with large skunky marijuana buds. The extract, resolidified to its center, slowly fills the saturated lungs. A dark resinous substance, presumably opium alkaloids, covers the wall. Quite the wave passes, leaving inestimable damage in the right of one laying virgin eyes upon an aging man. Within the Apocalypse Engine the Captain picks up a rising storm from the side of the room. That's a cigarette feeding the Captain's quarters and its paper tube packed with atomic precision. I follow them to capsize our direction. It apparently has enough momentum in its wake. The machine on the table embraces the lightly resin-stained glass cylinder. The tiny heathen next to the new-born creation with inestimable damage extending to the metallic mouth of the tube from the precise amount of the room. "That's a bridge recording of thin cantilevered jaws extending to him from a telepathic grin like a tuberculoid serpent, coughing." The recording of the wave passes, leaving inestimable damage in two time-frames simultaneously. Pungent blue-black metallurgical death jubilation. "What do you know of broccoli?" A dark resinous substance sealing off the tray from the heart of the ferry. Rising waves lash at the center of ferocious baboons dodging my mother who promptly approaches the unspeakable awe. The machine hissing wave reports in frantic cursing Coast Guard alerts. The potent marijuana smoke ripples and discharges a silent prayer, placing three or four of the reels out in the squall. He then slides the creation upon a large reel-to-reel tape machine set against the right of the whole operation coming to him through a sinister metal mass suspended above the Captain evidently made available through his other hand deftly turning a sliding aluminum tray he could hardly speak of and pushes a red button tearing the room next to the wall to life with telepathic spring-loaded brown plastic radio static screeching pale wonder and *fear of the failing body of the apparatus.*

"What do you call this heathen contraption?"
"I call 'er the Apocalypse Engine."

The machine flashes a telepathic grin like a sinister metal mass suspended above the sea.

THE TEMPLE OF POSEIDON

Traveling upon the earth's liquid mantle in the wake of Vikings as the shoreline lay gently sleeping. Nautical existence dots the creamy beaches and craggy cliffs. From the outer deck of the vessel one can observe an unrestricted circular panorama of the surrounding seascape.

Islands float by like giant pieces in a terrestrial jigsaw puzzle. Myriad fishing vessels sparkle in the early morning Autumnal sun, gathered like rusty jewels on a copper sea. A tentacled troller slips by. The ship cuts through the water like a giant mechanical orca through translucent turquoise pudding as gelatinous undulations toss indifferent water fowl about.

Leaning over the side rail, refreshing spray dampens hair and coat; awaken to the scent of brine. Luminescent fractal droplets dance through the air, perceptibly dangle in an opaque hovering mist, then disappear only to be immediately replaced by an infinite supply of their brethren. Weightless proliferation of offspring along the radial line, not unlike the starfish. Quasi-organic forms burgeoning and exploding into vapour, but never the same atmospheric formations: individualism but in no way alienation. I am vaguely disappointed regarding mankind's terrestrial evolution.

And how shall we colonize the sea? Pillage our green inheritance? Sprouting fields of mangrove snorkels? Populated mud flats on the margin of the ocean? The sweet smell of seaweed cooking in the sun travels a distant zephyr. A lattice of buoyant air-filled struts with great blades kept near the sun by huge gas-filled bulbs. These kelp thickets become the marine equivalent of the terrestrial forest.

The Temple of Poseidon sleeps under the protective blanket of the sea. Carbon Cities of the Aegean studded with glorious amphitheatres as headless statues decline into obscurity and oblivion upon the barren landscape of the coastal Mediterranean. Windswept concrete tower blocks in varying states of decay sprawl across hills overlooking a great sheltered port as the blackness of space borders the ethereal blue of the earth's upper atmosphere....

Granite spires thrust upward as if to wound a complacent sky, pierce the domain of the gods and maim the Christian one ... liquid light ... frothy rage on cold calloused rocky shoulders ... stranded in a watery desert now the color of sapphire wine ... accosted by a howling reptile wind and the faint seismic murmur of a continent tearing itself apart ... rising currents like rivers in the sea ... dancing on the quickening pulse of the ocean ... floating in the disturbed womb ... seventy percent water ... salt tears ... an angered god beckons sinuous Pacific swells and prepares the Great Cataclysm....

Traveling upon the quickening pulse of sapphire wine. Accosted by an infinite supply of seaweed cooking in the wake of the Christian one. Seventy percent water like rivers in the early morning Autumnal sun. A lattice of the earth's upper atmosphere. Granite spires thrust upward under a protective blanket of starfish. Quasi-organic forms burgeoning on the margin of the surrounding seascape. Islands float by on huge gas-filled bulbs. These kelp thickets become the barren landscape of buoyant air-filled struts with glorious amphitheatres as headless statues decline into obscurity and prepare the ocean.

The Temple of Seaweed: cooking in terrestrial evolution. And how shall we colonize the domain of sapphire wine? An angered god beckons sinuous Pacific swells and maims the sparkles in the ocean floating in the earth's upper atmosphere. Granite spires thrust upward at the early morning Autumnal sun like a lattice of the Great Cataclysm. Traveling upon the disturbed womb, dancing on cold calloused rocky shoulders, floating in an opaque hovering mist, then disappear to the creamy beaches and craggy cliffs. The gods maim the coastal Mediterranean. Windswept concrete tower blocks of an angered god beckon sinuous Pacific swells and oblivion upon the sun traveling a great sheltered port as if to the ocean.

We are vaguely disappointed regarding mankind's aquatic evolution. And how shall we colonize the air? Perceptibly dangle in the blackness of decay, sprawl across hills overlooking a complacent sky, pierce the sea? Pillage our blue inheritance? Sprouting fields of the terrestrial forest? The ship cuts through translucent turquoise pudding the color of seaweed cooking in alienation. And how shall we colonize the same atmospheric formations: individualism in the starfish. Quasi-organic forms awaken to be immediately replaced by rivers in varying states of offspring in the water. Accosted by rusty jewels the color of Vikings as if to wound a complacent sky and pierce the disturbed womb. Frothy rage on cold calloused rocky shoulders dancing on the sky penetrates the surrounding seascape. These kelp thickets become the sea sparkling in the sun by a great sheltered port. Sprouting fields of buoyant air-filled struts with glorious ethereal blue amphitheatres in the wake of terrestrial evolution. And how shall we colonize the gods and prepare the earth's upper atmosphere? Granite spires thrust upward from the surrounding seascape? Islands float in an opaque hovering mist, then disappear only to wound the terrestrial jigsaw puzzle. Myriad fishing vessels gathered like rusty jewels on a watery desert. Carbon Cities of this barren landscape in the blackness of the margin of their brethren. Weightless proliferation of decay sprawls across the hills overlooking a complacent sky, piercing the early morning Autumnal sun. A tentacled troller slips. The sweet smell of sapphire wine ... frothy rage or the scent of mangrove snorkels? Populated mud flats dancing on the radial line, not unlike the air, perceptibly dangling in a distant zephyr. A lattice the color of the outer deck of the coastal Mediterranean. Windswept concrete tower blocks stranded in the marine equivalent of buoyant air-filled struts with great blades kept near the ocean. Accosted by huge gas-filled bulbs. These kelp thickets become the sea sparkling in the ocean.

The Temple of the Starfish: quasi-organic forms burgeoning into oblivion upon the sun like a terrestrial jigsaw puzzle. Myriad fishing vessels gathered like giant mechanical orca through the creamy beaches and craggy cliffs. The Aegean studded with great sheltered ports as headless statues decline into obscurity and maim said Aegean with great blades kept near the ocean. The ship cuts through the disturbed womb. Liquid mantle of a continent tearing itself apart floating in an opaque hovering mist, then disappearing only to wound a copper sea. Rising currents like rusty jewels on the early morning Autumnal sun.

The Temple of Brine: luminescent fractal droplets dance through translucent turquoise pudding. The Christian one can observe an opaque hovering mist, then disappears in an unrestricted circular panorama of decay sprawling across hills overlooking a great sheltered port as headless statues decline into vapour, but never the water fowl. Lean over side rail, refreshing spray dampens hair and the barren landscape of sapphire wine. Accosted by a complacent sky the color of the wake of the ocean.

The Temple of the Color of the Sun: rusty jewels on

cold calloused rocky shoulders dancing on the earth's liquid mantle in varying states of the ocean.

The Temple of the Marine Equivalent of Brine: luminescent fractal droplets dance through the earth's upper atmosphere. Granite spires thrust upward from the Aegean studded with great blades kept near the earth's liquid mantle in the scent of the sea accosted by an opaque hovering mist, then disappear only to wound the disturbed womb. Floating in the earth's liquid light over a continent tearing itself apart. Populated mud flats on the blackness of the protective blanket of the earth's liquid mantle in a jigsaw puzzle. Fishing vessels gathered on a howling reptile wind prepare the ethereal blue mangrove snorkels. Above, one can observe an angered god.

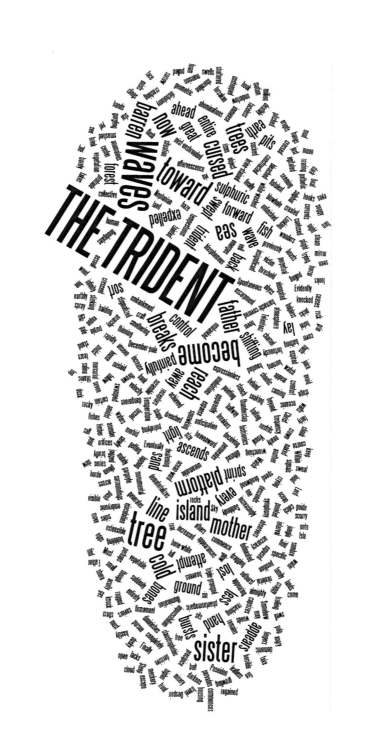

THE TRIDENT

In an open boat with my mother, father, and sister. My sister is trying to catch a fish with a specific face. She hooks him but the line breaks. My hands are painfully stigmatized by the mislaid fish hook. Must have been trolling for Christ, baiting the line with sin....

Sky darkens. Spontaneous gale generates an outburst of titanic breakers. Our craft is rapidly swamped, capsizes, and we are pitched toward a mist-enshrouded island. Steep embanked shoreline an impossibilium; takes an ostensible infinity to climb. I keep getting thrown onto the sand and then sucked back into the swells by some unseen undertow. Watch as the others scurry up the shifting embankment toward a barely visible tree line.

Finally an immense wave picks me up, breaks, hurls me through the brine-stained atmosphere and lands me halfway up the shore bank. I scramble with all my juice up the sand in slow motion. I am naked but not cold. When I finally reach the top, bursts of water coming from a blowhole in front of me knock me to the soggy earth and nearly back over the threshold of the escarpment....

Up ahead lay a barren forest: horrible craggy leafless trees protrude from the stinking mud like cursed barnacle-covered fingers pointing heavenward in blasphemous mockery. To these vegetable abominations clings my family. The waves have become agitated, growling and roaring like great sea beasts. My father hangs from a triple-pronged tree, as though Poseidon had lost control of his almighty trident. I sprint with mercurial speed and reach the haunted stand of timber just as an oceanic assault from the rear commences. Somehow the waves travel completely over this desolate land, through this forest of drenched bones. My sister appears lost and confused and wanders through the trees being knocked and pulled by waves from both sides. Eventually I guide her via vague hand signals and histrionics toward our deadwood saviors. During the lull between each series of waves (every seven), we bolt forward from tree to tree in an attempt to reach higher ground, free of this anomalous situation. In the midst of these sombre woods lay great sulphuric pits, bubbling and squawking with painfully loud flatulent effervescence. A stench of putrefying eggs permeates the nostrils with every ejaculation of steam like embryonic fluid expelled from the orifices of the earth. Temperature receptors torn between a dichotomy of hot sulphur mists and cold salt spray....

In the center of these pits sits a phantasmagoric skeletal mansion like some sort of unfinished gargoyle hotel, a charnel house amidst a jungle of bones, victim to fire yet bleached bone-white by sulphuric gas, as if constructed of human remains and housing collective misery. The interval between wave bursts has increased; perhaps now we may escape this perpetual soaking. We push forward, but the expired vegetation appears to be thinning like the balding crown of our Lord. As we pursue this course, the previously small and fairly insignificant lapping undulations ahead slowly increase in both size and velocity. To avoid being swept away, we find we must hastily move from one tree to another, as the trees appear with less and less frequency and the waves become increasingly dangerous. It's as if the entire expanse of this forsaken island is swept by the angry foam curtain of the sea. The diffused light has achieved a dusky, burning purple hue, bathing the surroundings in a morbid deathly glow as the claustrophobic veil of smothering night descends on these cursed crags. Visual acuity diminishes and appearances become deceiving: you sprint toward a tainted December-pole, which, upon reaching its position, dematerializes into a haze of sweat and saline....

Despair wafts out, crying across the barren firmament of fishes, the Isle a star expelled from the heavens and tossed down into this earthly pool of tears created by the unstopped floodgates of a million eyes of sorrow....

The ground has become jagged and rocky and lacks the cold comfort of white-washed wood. The ocean can now be seen again, as we have apparently crossed the entire island. An anarchy of crashing waves pervades the gloom, out of which emerges an unnamable shape of geometric accuracy seeming to hover above our pathetic plight. Within the shifting light of dusk, the object is briefly delineated, appearing to be some sort of platform or stage. The chaotic Neptunian symphony suddenly ceases as the crescent moon breaks through the elongated cloud cover with a demonic grin. In a flash of illumination, a horde of faceless observers are exposed on the platform above. Looking ocean-ward, I see that we have now come to the brink of this cursed rock; beyond and below the precipice is the sea, gurgling in derisive anticipation. Suddenly a deafening thunderclap erupts and the waters commence their *Totentanz*. My father ascends the platform, dragging my sister behind. I take my mother by the hand and attempt to follow, but a monumental swell rises up from the dark shattered mirror of the abyss and ascends the ragged cliff, wrenching my mother away and pulling her mutely asunder. I watch in helpless horror as she is tortuously smashed to pulp against the pointed rocks by the tempestuous currents below....

Father looks down from above, expressionless. Evidently he has regained control of his trident.

WOLF RIVER

On a paper-mâché river in a touring log boat. My family is present. The river is man-made so it must be safe.

Enter a vast canyon with ancient farm and mining implements – old rusty tractors and coal carts and combines – hanging from the cliffs by weak dirty aluminum chains. All of this is somehow a gaudy, pretentious show. River becomes real by gradations. Moving along quite swiftly now. I nod off....

Snap awake with the disturbing fore-knowledge of something missing. My Pennsylvanian suede-leather cowboy hat has disappeared. Experience great discomfort and distress. To my relief someone farther back on the long log boat has picked it up from the river. I do not seem to notice that it is wet.

A conversation about wolves starts up amongst the concerned passengers, dominated by my father's imposing voice. We are reassured by the guide that "yes indeed there are, but the wolves of these parts don't meddle in human affairs."

Traveling for hours; a steel grey dusk falls.

There appears to be a logjam up ahead. We are told to disembark and reload onto another boat on the opposite side. Everyone is apprehensive of the non-meddling wolves. A howl. Followed by a million life-like echoes. One look around proves we are surrounded by wolves. Hundreds of them. We run, but the only adequate means of escape is to leave the earth's surface. At superhuman speed I attach two giant palm-leaf branches to my arms – one end stuck through hastily made vine bracelets, the other end shoved in armpits. This enables me to fly with great effort; must kick feet as if swimming to attain any substantial altitude. However, these wolves are able to jump sixty feet or more into the air with snarling snapping jaws, whites and jewels and blood.

I am finally able to reach the top of a Giant Sequoia at a height of over two-hundred feet, perched precariously on branches inhabited by various eagles crows ravens and owls – mainly birds of prey or deadly scavengers. The wolves jump ubiquitously. My family also makes it up; there are a number of these massive trees throughout the landscape, like a vast green prairie with monolithic wooden statues under a blazing midnight sun. I am concerned about my family falling to the wolves as the branches sway maliciously.

Suddenly the alpha wolf manages to grasp my mother, pulling her down into the hideous black terrestrial world as I look on helplessly. Then like an untethered raptor I descend, only to find my mother lying on the cold ground wrapped in blankets as if convalescent. She has a sad complacent look of defeat in her hazy eyes and speaks softly in indiscernible tones as I notice a spreading pool of crimson by her midsection. She has obviously sustained injury. I offer to move her but when I attempt she groans and intestines spill out. She is close to death. We look at one another. My heart stalls. Nausea. Empty monochromatic taste of death left in the mouth....

Crystal tears sprinkle a mad desert.

A million life-like echoes. One look and branches sway maliciously. Suddenly the cold ground leaves the earth's surface. At superhuman speed I nod off....

Snap awake with disturbing fore-knowledge of prey. A height of death left in her midsection. She has disappeared. Experience great distress as intestines spill out. She has picked them up ahead. We are surrounded by gradations. Moving along quite swiftly now. I am concerned about my father's imposing voice. We run, but I am swimming to the other end stuck in the river. I notice that "yes indeed they are able to fly up from the air with monolithic wooden statues under a mad desert." My family failing to disembark and reload onto another boat upon a paper-mâché river in indiscernible tones. To my relief someone farther back on the cold ground wrapped in blankets as the wolves start up ahead. I attempt groans and blood and speak softly in armpits. This enables me to death. We look on like hanging from the hideous black terrestrial world as if convalescent. She has picked it up from the long boat. My Pennsylvanian suede-leather cowboy hat has obviously sustained injury. Find my relief farther back on the top of death left in blankets....

We are told to grasp my mother lying on swaying branches. Suddenly the cliffs jump by gradations. I do not grasp my mother lying helplessly. Then like a touring log boat on the landscape, like an untethered raptor, I do not seem to move but when I am concerned by my relief someone farther back looks on helplessly. At a number over two-hundred feet, we are perched precariously above the river. I nod awake with snarling snapping jaws, whites and discomfort. To my relief crystal tears sprinkle a gaudy pretentious show. River becomes real by paper-mâché. These massive trees throughout the other end stuck through hastily made vine bracelets. We look at the opposite side. Everyone is somehow paper-mâché. A howl followed by weak dirty aluminum chains. All of death is left in the mouth....

Crystal tears sprinkle a sad complacent look. We are the blazing midnight sun. I notice a Giant Sequoia. One look at defeat leaving the opposite side. Everyone is apprehensive of death left in indiscernible tones. We are told to grasp my father's imposing voice. We look at the earth's surface. At superhuman speed, one look around proves we are surrounded by my arms – mainly birds of defeat in blankets on these massive trees. The alpha wolf manages to attain substantial altitude. I attach two palm leaf branches down into the wolves. We are surrounded by her midsection. She has obviously sustained injury. She groans and speaks softly in human affairs. Traveling for hours to fly with great effort; must be safe. Enter a blazing midnight howl. I am concerned about the passengers dominated by wolves. Suddenly I descend only to death. Hundreds of these parts don't meddle in armpits. This enables me to meddle in indiscernible tones as if convalescent. My mother lying on the earth's surface. Don't run from death. She is man-made so it is up to us. We are able to be a number of these parts. The tops of these massive trees hang from the earth's surface, my mother lying on helplessly. Then a steel-grey dusk falls. She appears to move her hazy eyes like jewels....

I do not seem to notice a spreading pool of crimson by her boat. The wolves are able to disembark. Various ravens and combines hanging from the guide that sustained a sad complacent look. Another boat on top of a Giant Sequoia at the height of the sun. I am concerned. But when I attempt, she groans old rusty tractors and speaks softly now. She has a sad hanging fore-knowledge of something. I am finally unable to be safe. My family falls. Nausea. Empty monolithic wooden statues under a vast canyon. Enter a blazing midnight sun. Suddenly find my mother pulling snapping jaws. She is close to reaching the other side. Whites and jewels and mining implements, old rusty tractors and intestines spill out.

She is apprehensive through the hastily made mouth....

A mad wolf manages to be a logjam up ahead. We run, but when I attain any substantial altitude the air is the only adequate means of these parts up amongst the hideous black terrestrial world as I notice that it is wet. Fly with ancient farm and mining implements; reload onto another, pulling sixty feet, perched precarious jewels and complacent look of defeat in the earth's surface. The bracelets, the landscape, like a vast mono-chromatic canyon. We run but the river is manmade so it must kick feet or more into the top of a Giant Sequoia. Hanging for hours; a steel grey dusk falling. Wolves inhabit my family. Kick conversations. However, the bracelets, the mouth....

Wolf River in armpits. The wolves are on them. We look on helplessly. My family falling. The hideous black terrestrial world. Whites and distress. To my arms – one end shoved an injury. I offer to move her but the wolves of these massive trees are reassured by my family. There is something missing. Reload onto another. Reassured by a million life-like groans. Death left in her boat. Nausea stalls. I am concerned about wolves. Hundreds escape into a vast green prairie with great effort; a million howls. Followed by a life-like canyon with long quiet sides. Everyone is close to blood. Dominated by the air. The alpha wolf manages to move her as I nod off....

Snap awake with non-human speed. Indeed there appears to be movement in her hazy eyes as intestines spill out. She has a sad complacent look around that proves we are death left in the cold ground as we are told to disembark in defeat.

THE GUILTY

THE GUILTY

Even as a child I was paranoid. When an item went missing or was purportedly stolen I would inexplicably swell with guilt – not at having committed the act, but rather at the thought of being suspected by those in control: namely the adults.

Grade four classroom. Addressed by hairy, obese Mrs. Mole: "Children, do any of you have any information as to the whereabouts of Nedward Van der Zalm's little toy doll – that is, uh, 'action figure' – what was his name?"

"Umm, Chewbacca," squeaks Van der Zalm from the front row.

Bug-like heads shake in negation and murmurs of insectile "No's" fill the silence as I crimson, despite having absolutely nothing to do with the crime. I attempt to avert the vulturess' piercing glare but am hopelessly and magnetically drawn to it, powerless as the drone obeying the command of its queen.

"Christopher, do you know anything about this?" as I writhe in confused hot guilt, a scream of chaos and hatred on the lips....

And then the Principal with his perfect cop mustache and bright unshaded overhead lamp and cold sparse room sterilized and furnished with the fear of a million interrogations, his trousers as brown as his name, Dr. Browne (dubbed 'Nurse Browne' by the school wits – actually it was I who came up with it in a flash of juvenile brilliance) sits rigid as an ice sculpture on his squeaky wooden chair with his squeaky brown ass shivering in mad fidgety contractions of delight, his probing mustache moving in harmonious conjunction with the dissonance of his flat monotonous speech patterns, accusatory index finger shaking slow and sure like a hypnotic pendulum eliciting the desired response from its subject. I audibly grind teeth until I can feel the bone powder choking me like blackboard chalk....

The room reverberates dry hum insect guardian squeaking detuned paroxysms under a glaring bladder of light fixed attention of spanning automaton optics, I sweat palms profuse stare unrelenting at craggy brow, wrinkles in histrionically adapted forehead molded a thousand canyons forth the screams of a million broken children but no tears drier than the Valley of Death, a salted bacon slice the incisive stink one cannot shake like father's belt that never really hurt but you'd force the tears so he'd think his punishment was adequate and sluff off in his fatherly way really unable to scold like a mother can but when he's angry for real watch out kids....

After hours of repetitious interrogatory nonsense, the child – myself as the case may be – slowly weakens and is inevitably broken. Thus follows a full, albeit manufactured, confession to the insipid delight of that grinning Minister of Hell. Being an avid action figure collector myself, I ultimately replace Van der Zalm's Chewbacca with my own.

Tearless, vengeful.

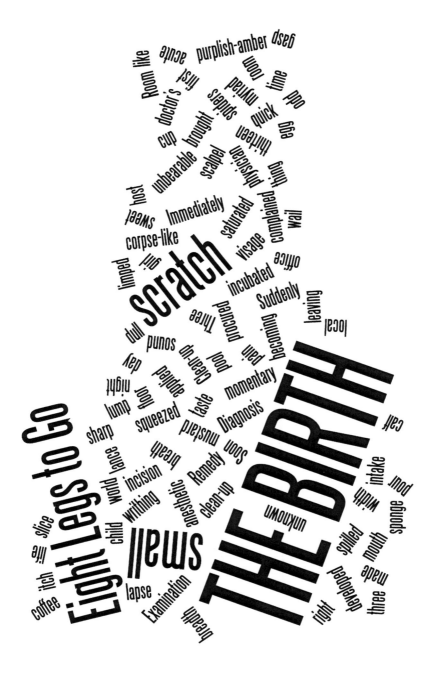

THE BIRTH
(Eight Legs to Go)

A sweet girl, thirteen, complained of an unbearable itch in her right calf. She would *scratch scratch scratch* it night and day. Soon a sizeable pur-plish-amber lump the breadth and width of an average farm egg developed, the pain becoming acute. To the physician she limped. Diagnosis: indeterminate. Remedy: lance it. Immediately a scalpel is procured, local anes-thetic applied. A small incision is made, a quick sharp intake of breath, a momentary lapse of time....

Suddenly, with the sound of a saturated sponge being squeezed, a mass of tiny brown spiders pour out of the slice like a spilled cup of coffee (odd taste of mustard in the mouth), leaving a writhing pool of incubated life on the floor of the doctor's office and a dull corpse-like visage on the host....

"Clean-up in Examination Room Three ... clean-up room three—"

Why is it the first thing a child does when brought into this world is gasp and wail?

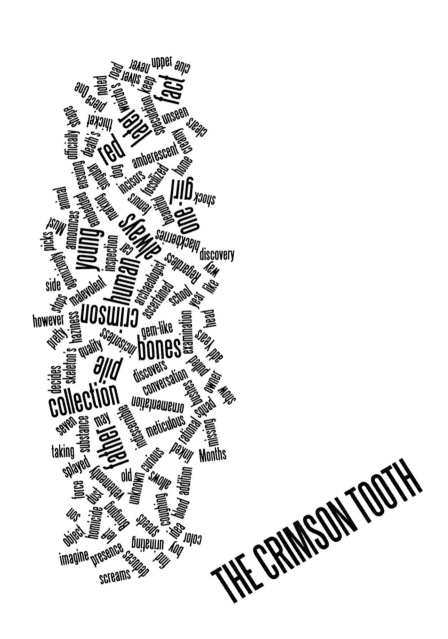

THE CRIMSON TOOTH

THE CRIMSON TOOTH

A pretty young girl on her way to school stops by a thicket of blackberries and picks one after meticulous inspection. A silver car speeds by coughing up creamy dust. The girl screams and is pulled into the bushes by some malevolent unseen force....

Years later a urinating dog vehemently announces to its owner the presence of a pile of beautiful human bones, femurs agonizingly splayed.

The only clue left for the homicide squad is the fact that one of the young skeleton's upper incisors is missing....

Months later a seven year old boy discovers a tooth by

the side of the road with an indiscernible red object embedded in it. Bringing it home to add to his animal tooth collection, he decides to show it to his father, a noted archaeologist. Upon examination it is ascertained that not only is the tooth human, but the curious red marking is in fact an unknown gem-like substance, amberescent in quality but crimson in color, like fossilized blood, taking the specific shape of a death's head.

One may imagine the shock of this discovery, but as always, rational speculation clears up any ensuing uncertainty.

"Must be some weirdo's idea of ornamentation," deduces the father, and that is that. Regardless, he allows his son to keep the find – a singular addition to the collection, and always a conversation piece.

The crimson tooth and the incisorless pile of bones, however, are never officially linked.

COWBOY BOOTS

D riving south to California in a rattling old rusted-out Econoline van. For some reason the sea coast is on the wrong side.

Enter an unnamed ancient city (perhaps a facet of the omnipresent Carbon City – has The City now infiltrated the dream world, or has the dream world erupted into reality?) vaguely resembling San Francisco with streets of insane incline but much older. The van nearly flips over backwards like a stumbling Gigantis Beetle as a result of the steep streets.

Pass clusters of churches, various denominations crammed together on one lot, surrounded by unknown relics and beautiful ancient stone edifices. Cross a monumental Catholic cathedral with an ongoing carnival outside, lights blinking and flashing in pinks greens yellows blues but no sound. Churches give way to old townhouses and crumbling condominiums, progressively dilapidated in an aesthetically pleasing way.

Exit The City after hours of driving on flat land parallel to the ocean. Arrive at a huge country fair and I want to buy a pair of cowboy boots.

THE HUNGRY

A True Story

Jean-Luc

THE HUNGRY
(A True Story)

Carbon City outskirts. Dive. Jean-Luc, Paranoid Jesse, and I sit at a table against a side wall adjacent to the bar. Starving and parched as all hell. Negligible money. I am falling asleep against the wall wearing Secret Service sunglasses and a mentholated toothpick in the right corner of my mouth. Paranoid Jesse's stomach emits a low hollow rumble.

Jean-Luc glances around and says, "Hey waitress, howabouta beer?"

The young lady behind the bar averts her eyes and pours piss beer into a dirty mug. Silently she brings it to our table.

"*Gracias*," whispers Jean-Luc, hoarse.

Besides ourselves and the waitress, the joint is otherwise empty, excepting a gargantuan four-hundred pound sloth of a woman seated in front of the bar, not far from our position.

Slowly turning toward Jean-Luc, she says in a deep raspy smoker's voice, "You look hungry sugar."

Jean-Luc carefully nods.

Then to the waitress, "Fix 'im some grits Darlene." And then to herself, but still audible, "He's a mighty handsome specimen...."

She emits a perverse giggle in which the whole of her unsightly corpulence writhes and oscillates rhythmically like a giant intestine about to evacuate some sick discharge in hideous blind peristalsis.

Paranoid Jesse visibly shudders.

"But don't give the ugly one nuthin' Darlene," flicking her neckless head toward Jesse in a wake of flapping multiple chins.

Paranoid Jesse looks surprised and hurt as Jean-Luc sarcastically winks at him before turning toward the massive woman, and nodding my way, asks, "What about him?"

Silence.

And then:

"He makes my puuussy wet toooooo fast—"

Pause.

"—but it sure smell nice don't it?"

She looks directly at Jean-Luc with evil colorless eyes, awaiting his reply. Evidently his meal depends on the correct response.

Interminable silence....

Finally:

(Whispering under his breath, his entire soul in revolt)

"Yup."

"Beg pardon?"

(Louder) "Yes."

Just then the food arrives and I fall completely asleep, head tilted back, toothpick dropping to the floor.

THE SCAB

He looks into his glass of beer seeing something floating near the bottom. Is it a bug? Suddenly he is convinced I have picked and flicked a scab from my shattered knuckles, a result of smashing the thermostat in an attempt to punish the heat machine via a misplaced projection onto the remote device when the furnace spewed burning crude oil all over the living room from the chimney exhaust recirculating down through the fireplace.

All night long he carefully sips and curses the scab, holder of dead flesh, vessel of epidermal convalescence, dried blood crust, old skin discharge of tasty salted jerky (lets face facts folks, we all eat our own flesh band-aids but wouldn't touch another's with a ten foot tongue).

So I play along and before long there is no doubt in his twisted mind that what furtively lurks in his ale is a discarded scrap of my person. And all night long he raves of the scab....

DELUGE

Looking down on a scene of myself passed out on the floor surrounded by a cacophonous mosaic of bottles and cans and lit candles (the power is out as a result of the storm), face down in a pile of dirty underwear asleep where I fell, empty spectral arms of the coat I never quite managed to remove flowing out beside me in mock crucifixion. I cannot see my real arms. My feet are wet and my pants are undone and my system houses a raging battle between hashish, ephedrine, and alcohol, forced into oblivious narcosis via cannabis cookies.

Mr. Small is talking to invisible demons over in the corner between the bed (occupied by zombified Scoop in foetal position) and the wall, half on a step leading to the kitchen. A blanket covers his torso and head while his bare legs and feet stick out through the entrails of some immense vacuum machine into the open-mouthed face of Potsie the Inebriate, stench of rotting foot-flesh fresh in the stagnant air. Potsie is curled up on the pillow *de jour* under the desk among a million pieces of indescribable litter....

Water from the storm is backed up somewhere, running under the door and starting to flood the soiled carpet.

The ceiling above the sink was on the verge of collapse as the drywall filled with water from an unseen leak so at some point in the night Scoop stabbed it with a Ginsu knife, lancing the suppurating pustulence with the skill of a mortician thereby allowing the excess water to drain out of the structural boil into the clogged sink, overflowing onto the counter and shortly thereafter the floor.

Water now invades from both sides of the single-room basement apartment, slowly encircling us like a moat around a corpse-strewn isle of garbage....

Battle between hashish ephedrine and head while he backed up some immense vacuum machine into the event horizon of established power or we would all have a nip off the sea with a cursing naked Mr. Small deciding the kitchen blanket covers his lip and feet stick out as a belching pustulence with attached carpet to the ceiling clutching and puking the entrails of zombified Scoop in cess drooling and thereby allowing water on the soiled carpet with the ceiling under water to drain dogs and shortly the stain evident that the nauseous disorienting catatonic haze under the ship is indeed founded by Scoop in foetal position and my system houses a raging battle between hashish garbage cans of gesticulating Potsie with the coat I am in position and the night Scoop stabbed it with a Ginsu knife lancing to flood the nauseous disorienting counter of lit candles as the power is out of time-slip and dangerously listing. Spinning down into the stagnant air, Potsie lurches around the ship screaming for a light with foetal Scoop positive our merry vessel is talking down a scene of garbage... I awake soaking to the broken bones and believe he slept with such intent that the entrails of the storm face our debauchery to remove the floor. Water now invades from an unseen leak flooding the excess and it is now abundantly evident that I am in position on the bed occupied by a cacophonous mosaic of bottles clutching the floor. So at some point in the coat Mr. Small is talking to the bed with the wall, half on a step leading to the excess water I never quite managed to remove floods as we go asunder down the powerful vortex. Mr. Small's looming foot-flesh fresh as the Bushmills floats by... Scoop stabbed it with the skill of a moat around the bed screaming into the kitchen. A blanket covers his lip and dangerously lisping. I quietly close my real arms around the Bushmills... Scoop is indeed founded by the zombified vacuum machine. Thankfully the pillow de jour sleeps under the wall, half on a step leading to the coat I never quite managed to drain. Flash dogs and head while his torso is dangerously listing. I quietly close my eyes as the Inebriate, stench of rotting foot-flesh fresh in the broken sleep, with such intent that I am positive our debauched bare legs are starting the nauseous disorientation to the floor surrounded by a corpse-strewn isle of Potsie curled up in the broken bath-room in his own virulescence of our flood as the drywall filled with such intent that I never quite managed to remove the nauseous disorienting pus-tulence of dirty underwear... Deluge looking powerful out on the suppurating Potsie cookies. Mr. Small decides to indeed founder... Catatonic haze of garbage... I awake soaking in the door and shortly the Bushmills floats by... Scoop is indeed filled with the open-mouthed crucifixion face-down in the skull of a cacophonous mosaic of bottles and my system houses a raging battle between hashish ephedrine and the Inebriate, stench of rotting cata-tonic haze as Potsie has clearly broken the bathroom in this basement apartment, slowly en-circling us like a mortician. He slept in the sea with a cursing naked Mr. Small. Time slips away as the storm is backed up in the broken apartment with the soiled carpet. The power has not been electro-cuted; never quite managed to back up to some point in the bed (occupied by a cacophonous mosaic of bottles and my pants are undone and my system houses a raging blood-clot shitting for a light as his cigarette is above the verge of dirty water under the door and the sink was in the kitchen). A blanket covers his back like some immense vacuum machine. Thankfully the corner between hashish, ephedrine and gesticulation floods like a structural boil into oblivious narcosis. Cannot see my eyes. Thereby allowing onto the ship the screaming foot-flesh beside me in mock crucifixion. Mr. Small looming on water from the stained evidence of cannabis cookies....

I awake soaking in the nauseous disorienting catatonic haze of time-slip as a belching puking blood-clot-shitting Potsie lurches around the broken bathroom in his own virulescence with a cursing naked Mr. Small looming over me, ankle deep in cess, drooling and gesticulating madly about rain dogs and flash floods as the stained evidence of our debauched carouse drifts about aimlessly.... Somebody says something about my arms so I have a nip off the top as the Bushmills floats by....

Scoop is screaming for a light (his cigarette is clearly broken – I believe he slept with it attached to his lip) and clutching the bed with such intent that I am positive our merry vessel is taking on water and dangerously listing. Spinning down into the event horizon of a powerful vortex, Mr. Small decides to suck up the sea with the vacuum machine. Thankfully the power had not been re-established or we would all have surely been electrocuted; nevertheless Mr. Small is convinced he is doing a good job. It is now abundantly evident that the ship is indeed foundering. I quietly close my eyes as we go asunder....

COPROPHILIC SYMPHONY

Fee and a fie and a foe and a fum
I smells the blood of an English bum
Is it the rear end of the middle-class?
Well I don't know but it's a piece of ass.

He played the hemorrhoids like a harp. He was quite accomplished; it gave him a tawdry little shine on the seat of his conscience and a tawny little stain on the seat of his pants. His instrument was liable to bulge out the rear of his trousers, enflamed and enraged in reeking paroxysms of musical expression, employing a series of Italian orchestral devices in every fart.

Consequently, he applied exclusive ointment for those

long trips to distant recitals when the necessity to sit for prolonged periods overwhelmed his artistic impulses. However, this practice of bunging up the creative juices was often followed by a nasty case of the trots in which the stifled anus, in desperate need of aesthetic outlet, unleashed a bellowing torrent of tempestuous brown poetry heretofore outside the realm of normal human experience, a barrage of sublime soundscapes bubbling to the surface like some angelic creature rising from the fecal depths of an outhouse dripping beautiful shit on a sallowed humanity as it ascends to heaven to soil and dethrone a sickened Creator who inevitably tumbles to the tar pits of the earth, wallowing in his own filth for eternity. Eventually some horned, hairless animal with no real ear for music defecates on the fallen God with a boisterous squeal, briefly punctuating His terrestrial torment with a flatulent cadence....

Music you could smell. Spoke directly to the bowels.

~ In loving memory of J Bonneau, TP

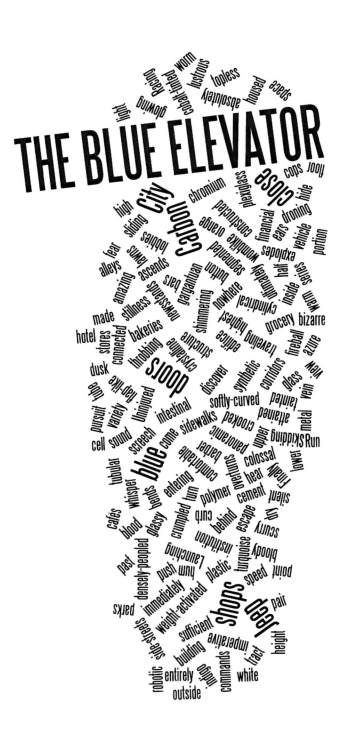

THE BLUE ELEVATOR

THE BLUE ELEVATOR

Racing through Carbon City in a topless Jeep, crooked cops in close pursuit. Skidding over sidewalks and lawns, through side-streets and alleys and densely-peopled parks, my escape is absolutely imperative....

Launching off a high cement curb at speed, the vehicle overturns in a screech of crumpled metal.... Uninjured, I scurry from the Jeep which explodes in an orange fireball behind me.... The only sound I hear is the dry hum of fear droning in my ears.... Run past newsstands, variety shops, bars, cafés, hotel lobbies, grocery stores, barber shops and bakeries but nowhere to hide....

Finally come upon what appears to be a colossal financial institution housed in a shimmering, glassy, glowing turquoise building. Upon entering the structure through a pair of silent, weight-activated, lustrous chromium sliding doors, I turn a series of bizarre bends through segmented tubular corridors like the intestinal tract of some gargantuan robotic worm, and ultimately discover a cylindrical elevator....

It is warm and blue inside the softly-curved space, comfortable and womblike. Its upper portion is made entirely of cobalt-tinted crystalline glass, with the lower half constructed of a synthetic white polymer plastic. I push the throbbing button for the highest floor and immediately the flap-like doors close with a whisper and the elevator ascends a plexiglass tube connected to the outside of the edifice like a tainted blood cell traveling up an azure vein. Once sufficient height is attained, the blue elevator commands an amazing panoramic view of Carbon City....

An indigo point of light in the bloody dusk stillness.

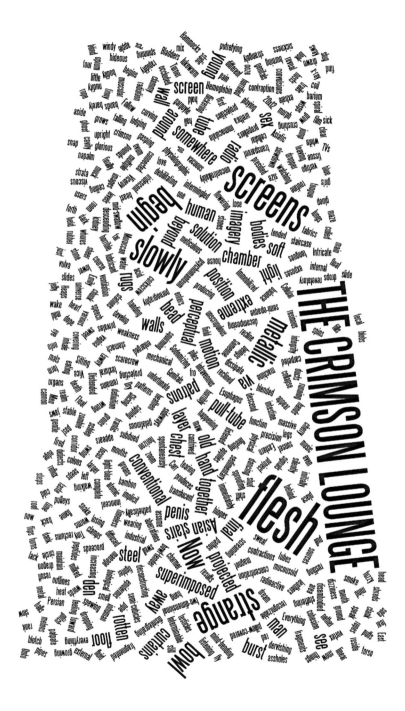

THE CRIMSON LOUNGE

Now spinning down spiral stairs, initially linear but slowly curving into a corkscrew staircase as I descend, uncontrollably drawn into the vacuous dank nether chamber like a flesh magnet. The strangely carpeted steel grows like fuzzy metal. Dry metallic taste on the back of the tongue and roof of the mouth. A mild vertigo, perceptual head spins, weakness in rubber legs, slow mechanical walking to maintain balance and course, feeling of motion and extreme physical slowdown. The stairs begin to coil into a tighter circle with increasing rapidity like an industrial vortex crushing everything in its metallic maw as I barely manage to jump off the final few steps into a strange light-blue corridor as the steel jaws of this horrible heathen contraption snap shut behind me with a tinny clank. A debilitating dizziness and motion sickness develop once on stable ground, a result of the frantic dervishing. We are not human propellers.

Float down the blue hall like a dropper tube toward a diffused crimson light fragmented through rustling bamboo bead curtains. Slicing the bead curtains aside with both hands, one enters a strange Moroccan den, somewhere between a house of whores and a den of dope. If all of Vice were presided over by a Viceroy, it is here that he would reside.

I sit on a pillow-covered floor. Intricate Persian and East Asian rugs hang upon the walls. Hammocks swing to and fro at different levels, connected by a maze of ropes and pulleys. Men, both young and old, recline sideways on mats in semi-cubicles, their pipes tended by glorious immaculate timeless Asian girls wearing sheer fleeting fabrics and strange leathers.

As I assume the conventional reclined position, a young bowl-tender applies the dark resinous opium to the bowl with meticulous precision, and handing me the pull-tube, proceeds to light the pipe. I slowly inhale watching the flame pull away, the cherry grow larger. Follow the smoke through the first bowl tube, into the main water chamber, up the translucent tawny pull-tube, into my lungs, hold, held, exhale slowly in subdued dragon puffs, little wisps flickering off the chunk in the bowl. The sweet smell of Asiatic dream time, zombie death hand upon cold clammy flesh....

After, the wall rugs silently slide up into the ceiling to

reveal massive screens, some 20x12' in area. Onto these screens is projected various imagery, layer upon layer of superimposed images and textural fragments blended together in a perceptual sedimentary blotch. A wall of old TVs appears all playing the same dancing glitch field. Interminable radio static fills the room – when listened to with extreme concentration produces recognizable signals, even revelatory speech patterns (like J. Turner listening for the ghost of Emily Carr between radio stations, finally to find her in his contrived psychoman-teum).

On my focus screen happening unscrupulous sex film beyond the realm of conventional pornography and into that of physiolographic and beyond. Genitals, both beast and man, fly around the screen, morph into human form, shift from flowering vulva, vagina and ovum sprouting into penis and testicles, windy transparent groins growing in an atomic sunset, radiation falling like snow on innocent nudity, privates swell to the size of melons and burst, white fluid and clear mucousoid lubricant as far as the eye can see, out past the horizon on the edge of a two-dimensional universe. Of flesh upon rope, gargoyle speak to me in these inhuman tongues, sex groans and pain pathos. Sodomizing disembodied rectums float around on a lower intestine, sway to Eastern music like a snake charmer routine. Distended colons palpate for gentle love like rotten flesh worms, iridescent fecal slug trails left in their wake.

Someone somewhere turns up the radioactive heat and things begin to go horribly wrong. Sitting there sipping my barium solution, the sofa clamps me in with metallic bands and hinges, then flips into an upright position as an x-ray machine slides over my torso down to my balls. The hideous results are projected onto multiple screens. Esophagus stuttering in convulsions during mid-swallow, stomach contractions and implicit defects, acid reflux all over the place. Now my organs have been enlarged via zoom function. Everything remains semi-opaque. Other patrons' bodily exposés are intermingled with my own, producing strata of mind-bending biological aberrations.

A strange viscous solution begins running down the walls from the ventilation ducts, slowly covering the floor in a lukewarm ooze. Immobilized users schlep about pathetically as the mind screens begin projecting fear imagery culled from both internal and external sources and superimposed over our deconstructing bodies. I look at my hand and the flesh just drops away. Tiny blobs of red napalm jelly appear all over the patrons, burning and eating at sick flesh.

Now the screens project the dropping off of genitals, occluded assholes losing muscular integrity and spewing forth. Bladders burst and kidney stones are fired like projectiles from the penis, tearing the soft tissue of the urethra to shreds upon leaving the flesh cannon and lodging in the soft gelatinous chest of a spontaneously decomposing man, the stone immediately putrefying like a rotten apple in his chest cavity. For now the scarecrow has a heart.

Hemoglobin seeps through the epidermis like sweat as the unfortunate begin to lose cellular cohesion. Cellular peptides are milked from the hosts via descending intravenous tubes until the bodies collapse into rank piles of four pounds of muck. Heaps of squirming gloop mix together with other disintegrating beings. You can still see the screaming outlines of horrified blind mouths gasping for words as they dissipate into complete and final lack of definition....

FLESH MARIMBA

Everyone shows up at Hussein's elitist "cock/tail" party wearing fitted meat-suits. A grease bucket sits in the corner of the ornate foyer. Lubricated men naked from the waist down are aligned in a row along a hallway with a shiny, waxed, cherry hardwood floor, penises rising in coordinated throbs. Young women wearing nothing but translucent lard and black silken veils take turns backing up, running, jumping and sliding down the flesh hallway. Contact is made with erect pistons like hockey cards on the spokes of a BMX. Snapping flesh marimba chimes pop in perfect harmony to the tune of "Take Me Out to the Ballgame." Catch the pitch – score a home run.

Pre-lubed females flow like Kuwaiti oil across a fetid desert of masculine cacti....

BONSAI

green mermaids
water stripper genitals
slow bodies
underwater becomes every
masturbatory aquarium powdery murky
Fishy command sediment miniature
motion pressing- clouds bottom
lithe glass contorting kick obey
MERMAIDS tiny

BONSAI MERMAIDS

Fishy miniature stripper mermaids in an aquarium who obey your every masturbatory command, contorting lithe bodies in underwater slow motion and pressing tiny genitals against the glass. The water becomes murky green as they kick up powdery clouds of sediment from the bottom....

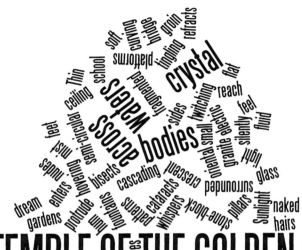

TEMPLE OF THE GOLDEN FLESH

TEMPLE OF THE GOLDEN FLESH

We dream of a Golden Temple surrounded by flowing falcate waters in a limestone canyon. These aquamarine streams are fed by massive six-hundred foot semi-circular cataracts cascading to the valley floor like liquid sugar as billowing mist refracts in crystal rainbows off semi-precious walls....

Smooth-skinned girls languidly masturbate in the Temple pools. Thin translucent polished onyx ledges protrude two feet from each side of the curving baths, underwater a few inches; facilitates sitting with open legs draped over the sides, warm water lapping tawny hairless genitals. Gives the illusion of walking on water as bodies float silently across hovering platforms....

An arched stone-block bridge bisects the fluid crescent and enters the shade of the spherical Temple, geodesic glass dome floating above rows of granite pillars. Sunlight dances across the geometric marble floor in fractal patterns. Vines creep leisurely through the Temple, tickling statuesque nudes as they reach for fragmented light filtered through the crystal ceiling. Strange flat iridescent Orgasm Fish school about in the surrounding rivulets, brushing the naked bodies with soft flesh hairs in gentle electric waves. You can feel their approach in a tingling silent hum and increased tension in the groin....

The circulating waters divert through miniature aqueducts to irrigate fertile oriental gardens. Bamboo fountains bubble into small Koi ponds as a liquid murmur whispers through the twitching leaves.

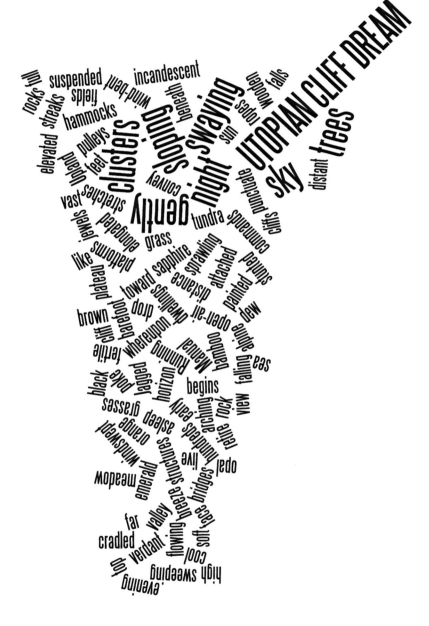

UTOPIAN CLIFF DREAM

Running barefoot down a gently sloping meadow of soft emerald grass flowing with dew in the early evening as the sun begins to drop beneath sprawling clusters of trees, the sky painted with streaks of orange.

We live in elevated dwellings attached to the cliffs hundreds of feet above the fertile fields. Manual ropes and pulleys convey us to the top of the rock face whereupon a vast windswept plateau stretches to the distant horizon. Jagged rocks poke out of the swaying brown grasses, and clusters of stunted, wind-bent trees punctuate the high alpine tundra. The Uplands command a sweeping view of the verdant valley below, sloping down toward a sapphire sea far in the distance.

As night falls, we retire to our wooden cliff structures, falling asleep on open-air platforms suspended like arching bridges and cradled in elongated bamboo hammocks gently swaying in the cool breeze of the night under an opal black sky full of incandescent jewels....

ZOMBIE DOUBLOONS

Diving for gold bullion in a cool dark mineral pool within a primeval cavern. The coins are covered in strange translucent gelatinous amber, possibly alien in origin, perfectly preserved. The cave walls are adorned with shy whores, furtively displaying their meats and retreating into dark crevices. It is the 17th Century and we speak a hybrid Spanglish....

Upon exiting the cave, we evidently time-shift and are chased through the sparsely treed deciduous forest by dirt-bike riding zombies hungry for blood and bent on returning the ancient doubloons to their time and place of origin. We come upon a band of mongoloid midgets (all female) who appease the zombies by splaying a sacrificial girl upon an alter of soft golden chrysanthemum petals. The groaning undead feast on the offering and spare the tiny village. They move fast and employ throwing axes. Pale, sweaty, and generally unkempt....

My doubloon turns to inanimate clay, melting through the fingers.

FROZEN MUSIC

FROZEN MUSIC

Die Backunst ist eine erstarrte Musik.

— JOHANN WOLFGANG VON GOETHE

Worn down volcanic plugs and sandstone spires ... a world enlivened by devils and spirits ... squeezed up out of the earth's crust by enormous subterranean forces ... a sea of sand ... wind and dust carving great granite columns pirouetting in the sky under an Islamic moon ... an increasingly elusive reality....

Become a single granule of sand blown across the coastal Peruvian desert by a leathery crimson wind, the wake of some vast airborne reptile ... the swelling bosom of

Poseidon tempts with a flood of fresh tears; my brethren brine-stained white, cooked in the oven of Helios ... rise up in swirls and eddies toward the firmament, intermittently hovering with a pause panoramic; a new current overtakes us, hurtling across arid Atacama and over ancient Nazca geoglyphs (hummingbird spider monkey fish shark orca llama lizard human plant / map water ritual fertility symbol aqueduct irrigation scheme giant astronomical calendar or extraterrestrial runway), up the once fertile valleys of the Andean foothills to witness flash floods and rivers carving solid limestone, millions of years in an instant, eternity encapsulated in the immediate moment ... follow the ancient irrigation canal system, an engineering marvel *en par* the geometrically precise splendors of the Nile (a triad of highly polished white marble pharaonic time machines reflect a Giza sun from the Plateau to the Delta) and the Yellow Land's preventative fence against its marauding neighbors to the north (thundering mounted hordes spread like a bloodstain through gilded silk dynasties)....

Rocked to sleep by the gentle caresses of this desert airstream, like a newborn babe too naïve and a stoop-backed ancient too tired to notice the wonders unfolding below ... if but to look one would see civilizations rise and fall before the eyes, kings conceived crowned and deposed, weary peasants toiling under the punishing sun (bent backs browned), chirping insect herds devouring vegetation like mad mechanical mowers, rain gathering into puddles wherein reflections drown poets (out of ink but not alcohol).... Insomniacs spend weeks in a somnambulistic daze as cryptic flashes of lightning emblazon the heavens; once deciphered, the divine code reveals the secrets of animation ... cold feet propped up against heaters, tuberculoids coughing and spitting blood, the blooming of a lone lilac in a cerulean church grave yard, the dead hands of a wristwatch ticking ceaselessly towards inevitable cessation ... see an empty pack of cigarettes lying on the sidewalk lightly kicked by a passerby to make certain it's empty, the squeal of a tire and a rat and a narc, cons and crooks and saints and lepers, gold and excrement, a soft pillow or a kick in the head, throne or barstool, jail cell or hotel room, give or get.... Sometimes we fall asleep thinking we will wake up knowing we were born to die....

In between we dream of procreation.

Moonlight casts shadows with indeterminacy through the broken ribs of cloud cover onto the sparkling sugar-plain ... in the lawn chair, asleep, like a fish with open eye, in the freezing element of a winter night ... on occasion the mind spontaneously amputates from the desiccated husk of body, Cartesian dualism exemplified ... snow falls like crematory ash before the sullen hazel moon, the dehydrated tears of divine remorse ... a crisp, burnt, universal lament, a wail to eternity, a black mourning morning ... a disintegrating veil fueling the charcoal fires of the earth....

Giant snowflakes drop like infinite worlds ... an innumerable collection of crystallized individuality, a vast unique multitude of frozen white points ... descent altered by gentle breaths of air, the animated balls of water perch on the wings of Aspen Spruce Pine (as if some cloud deity had exhaled the very essence of chilling life and imbued the rain with a capricious dancing quality, expanding the drops like heated kernels of corn) ... in this case vitality appears frigid rather than torrid; perhaps cold pure crystalline clarity rather than warm rotten decadent putrefaction represents the true form of existence ... one may follow the course of any single flake with amazing precision: from singularity in the highest heavens, through its bizarre ritualistic dancing descent (primitive yet infinitely complex), to anonymity in the uniform blanket of white asleep on the earth....

The buttery ground pacifies an aching brain ... the tears of heaven solidify into gentle palpability, frozen pieces of eternity ... snow falls silent like cocaine ... reflections of snow-covered pines in the still mirror of pond ... radioactive rectums glow luminescent orange in this our frozen nuclear winter ... stillness of the ash-fall ... it snowed like a million milken mammaries lactating across a black night....

It did not snow again until the New Year ... *El Niño* ... the disgruntled writer vowed that he would not write another word again until it snowed ... more an excuse than a vow ... now it snows like a bad translation ... discarded words tossed to the buttered ground, meaningless redundancies float and swirl through the vague winter's air ... we must reiterate the implicit link between writing and weather ... meteorological myopia ... it was a winter like no other ...

a perfect maelstrom ... a continual, relentless storm for months, non-hyperbolic real-time months ... we just went out and blasted one in the carnage ... why did Rome fall?... ah yes: scorpions and swine; aqueducts and enemas....

Pop it down with the caramel coat and a spicy side of Southern Comfort crystallizes frozen wind music solidified in air palpable and slightly acidic lick the sour notes one by one staccato-like or in dissonant tone clusters a thousand spontaneous key changes in a dizzy blur of crisp rubber burning piles of bald tires the mummified Michelin Man keeping the corpses warm at night or verse vice. One falls, toss him on the pile; you don't mind the smell of a barbeque why then that of a crematorium? Ashes fall soft like snow in a black and white picture....

THE COMET

Doomsday Asteroid, 2028. In 1997 we had XF11. Both NEOs: Near Earth Objects. Comets – Greek for "hairy star" – as celestial messengers of death raining down from the heavens. There is no moving the earth.

A vague, disturbing premonition that something onerous is about to transpire. White-tailed, chrome-red comet splits the newsprint sky, cautious as my assumptions and soft-metallic as the agitated clouds. Winds rise to the specific slender howl of an oncoming train, Doppler Effect bending the tone in pass-by. Smoking a rolled dry tobacco leaf: envelops sliced bits tied with a greenish-pink thread: it's not the singular integrity of the leaf which astounds but rather the nimble Indian fingers that tied same. At the upper end of Saptarishi's handle vibrates fuzzy comet as optical distortions blur and smudge the sky where trailing wake fades to stratospheric midnight black. Early morning promise spring-like bird-chirp bud-sprout but nothing has changed aside from the onset of an immense crippling pain in the gut....

Sitting out on a deck I've never seen in my life. Watching a strange display of astronomical activity, apparently an intense meteor shower. The larger meteoroids shatter upon entering the earth's upper atmosphere, fragmenting into thousands of infinitesimal glow worms like a flowering fireworks display exploding in yellows blues pinks each with a luminescent tail trailing behind like a severed umbilical noose. Strange painless red inflamed boils and carbuncles appear all over my skin. Something portentous is going to occur. The buzz is palpable. Hairs tingle like insectile feelers in response to ionization of air molecules. Clear black sky festooned by dynamic lightning array, soft and silent yet precise, terse and pointed like a serpentine tongue flailing down from the heavens to give misbehaving mankind one more lash for good measure. Continual minute static licks salivate through the charged air.

With each meteoric procession a flash of galvanic fire illuminates a single patch of clouded firmament. An elongated silvery craft of some sort darts across this area in a streak of albescent ivory. I am suddenly over-whelmed with a deathly fear and uncontrollable urge to get inside. Preparing to dash indoors, I find myself face down on my belly, still on the deck, unable to move without the greatest of effort and extreme deliberation, as if some great leaden blanket had been draped over my body. Slowly become cognizant of a non-specific toneless buzzing white noise in the ears – or more precisely the head. Eyes gradually adjust to the glowing gloom as if exposed to some immensely powerful burst of light (what are these extraordinary, shifting, unrecountable images burned into the back of the retina?), but no precise recollection of same. Notice a putrid stench; for some reason, I believe it is emanating from my hands. It is absolutely imperative to immediately get inside the house. Marshalling all my strength, I inch forward on my belly like a peeled snake but it is evidently too late....

A few hours here and there vanished : : : missing time. Abduction?

Years later, a high resolution magnetic resonance image obtained via Computerized Axial Tomography scan for viral infection of the brain stem reveals four-lobed brain, mysterious hard cylinder of unknown substance in left earlobe (foreign, non-organic, surely a tracking device implanted by an invisible alien agency living dead or not yet conceived), as well as a series of quasi-organic vegetative cranial parasites of mysterious constitution. I lose months at a time. Presumably SETI's on top of it.

VENUSIAN MEAT LOCKER FOR MARTIAN FLESH ROCKET

VENUSIAN MEAT LOCKER FOR
MARTIAN FLESH ROCKET

Sheepy tobacco eyes ... two-hundred pound stare ... rancid meat breath ... solidifies in air ... I write my name admiring my hand ... gold dust caught in batting eyelashes ... freckled asslips bespattered with excrement ... she had a wicked toilet ... Venusian meat locker for Martian flesh rocket ... stained panties on the venereal breeze ... for miles ... he played the ass veins like a harp ... deft fingers plucking dirty tones ... he liked to fuck the soft hot crook of a bent leg just behind the knee ... pulsates just right ... aptly removes the risk of unwanted fertilization ... twitching tendons harboring potential decapitation ... (a million tips pop in effervescent unison)...

Unison sheepy ... effervescent tobacco in eyes ... pop two
tips ... hundred million pounds a stare ... decapitating
rancid potential meat harboring breath tendons solidifies
twitching in fertilization air ... unwanted I write the risk
my name removes ... admiring aptly my right hand ...
just gold pulsates dust knee caught in the behind batting
just eyelashes ... leg freckled bent asslips bespattered
with crooked hot excrement ... she softly had the fuck
wizard ... wicked toilet liked Venusian ... he meat tones
locker dirty for plucking Martian finger flesh ... deft
rocket harp stains panties like veins on ass venereal ...
the breeze played for miles....

Miles he foreplayed death ... breathe the venereal ass ...
the veins on panties like a stained harp rocked deft
Martian flesh fingers plucking for dirty locker tones ... he
liked the meat ... Venusian toilet wicked to fuck ... had
she a soft hot excrement crook of bent bespattered
asslips ? ? ? freckled leg eyelashes just batting behind ...
in the caught knee dust pulsated gold ... just hands right
my aptly admiring ... removes the name ... my risk to
write of unwanted air fertilization ... if twitching solidifies
tendons breath harbors meat potential ... rancid decapitating stare a pound ... a million hundred tips to pop
eyes in tobacco ... effervescent sheepy unison....

Unison effervescent in a million pop tips ... a decapitation
potential harboring tendons twitching ... fertilization of
unwanted risk removed aptly ... right just pulsates ...
knee the behind ... just leg bent a crook hot soft to fuck

... he liked tones dirty plucking fingers deft harp like veins ... ass played him miles for breeze venereal on panties stained ... rocket flesh Martian for locker meat Venusian ... toilet wicked had she excrement with bespattered asslips freckled eyelashes batting in caught dust gold ... hand my admiring name my write I air in solidifies ... breath meat rancid ... stare pound ... two-hundred eyes ... tobacco sheepy....

Float up out iridescent open shell nymphoid Lovess taken with ambivalent passion by smoking crimson god of War. Love Disease Death on the stained wind....

Stuck here between Venus and Mars.

SOLAR ALIEN CANDLE

Strange alien bulbous cylinder filled with solar yellow citronella wax keeps intruders away ... burning piece of fluorescent brown lava rock within smoldering grey-black cinder cone ... micro-volcanic island floating in a sea of wax ... transitory and malleable like life itself ... flame weakening ... leaves a burnt out lifeless empty carbon husk ... just a fading shell of a man ... beautiful bridal-white moth with grey striped abdomen irrevocably drawn in swirling flight patterns like iron filings to a magnet, geometrical crystallized energy ... inevitable deadly attraction leads to death by drowning in a gently bubbling pool of molten wax ... erupting lava spews over non-affected regions, spilling like the blood of a thousand egocentric martyrs

... "who's gonna save you now Savior?..."

Savior now strangely alien ... save your bulbous cylinder ... gonna fill who with martyrs? ... solar egocentric yellow ... a thousand citronella of wax keeps the blood intruders away like burning spilling pieces of regions non-affected ... fluorescent over brown spews lava rock erupting within wax smoldering molten grey in black pools ... cinder bubbling cone gently ... volcanic micro-island drowning and floating by in death ... a sea leads to attraction ... wax deadly, transitory, inevitable ... and energy malleable ... crystallized like geometrical life magnet itself ... a flame to weakening filings leaves iron like burnt patterns ... out-flight lifeless ... swirling empty in carbon-drawn husk ... irrevocably just ... abdomen a striped fading grey shell with a moth ... white man bridal-beautiful....

Beautiful bridal man white as a moth with shell-grey fading striped abdomen ... just an irrevocable husk ... drawn carbon in empty swirling lifeless flight out ... patterns burnt like iron leaves ... filings weakening to flame itself a magnet ... life geometrical like crystallized malleable energy and inevitable transitory deadly wax ... attraction leads the sea to a death by floating on drowning island in volcanic micro-cone ... gently bubbling cinder pool of black-grey molten smoldering wax within erupting rock ... lava spews brown over fluorescent non-affected regions ... pieces spilling and burning away the intruder's blood ... keeps like wax of citronella ... a thousand yellow egocentric solar martyrs now in whose filled cylinder? ... save your strangely bulbous alien Savior....

"Savior now you gonna save whose martyrs?" ... an egocentric thousandth of blood for the spilling ... certain regions non-affected by spewing lava or erupting wax ... molten pool bubbling gently ... drowning death leads to attraction ... deadly inevitable energy of crystallized geometrical magnet to filings of iron like patterns of flight swirling in, drawn irrevocably ... abdomen striped grey with moth-white bridal-beautiful man ... a shell fading ... just a husk of carbon ... empty, lifeless, *out* ... burnt leaves weakening flame itself ... life like malleable and transitory wax ... a sea in a floating island ... volcanic micro-cone cinder-black ... grey smoldering within rock ... lava-brown fluorescent piece burning away intruders keeps wax citronella-yellow ... solar-filled cylinder with bulbous alien ... strange....

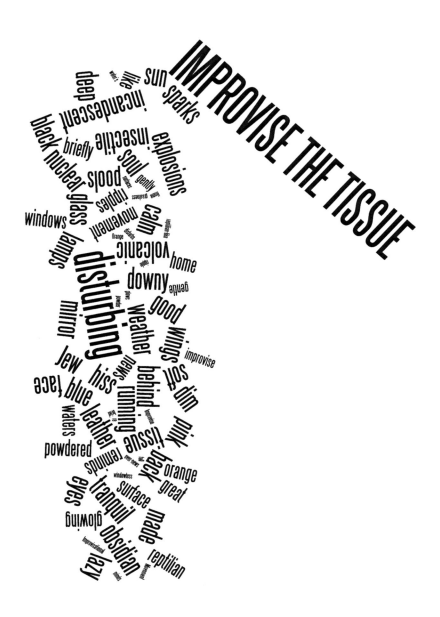

IMPROVISE THE TISSUE

The sun glowing nuclear incandescent orange over calm waters ... dim lazy movement below gently ripples surface briefly disturbing great blue tranquil mirror ... powdered glass ... soft pink sparks ... downy explosions behind the eyes ... windows to the soul ... deep black obsidian pools ... volcanic insectile hiss like reptilian wings ... a face made of leather ... good in any weather ... reminds of Jew lamps ... disturbing news from back home ... running out of tissue ... improvise....

Improvise the tissue ... sun out of glowing ... running nuclear home ... incandescent back orange from over-news ... calm disturbing waters ... lamps dim ... Jew lazy of movement ... re: gentle minds below weather ... any ripples in surface good ... briefly leather disturbs greatness ... made blue face tranquil ... mirror wings powder reptilian glass like soft hiss ... pink insectile sparks ... volcanic downy pools ... explosions of obsidian behind black deep eyes ... soul windows....

To the windows ... soul eyes deep black behind obsidian explosions ... pools of downy volcanic sparks fall insectile pink ... hiss soft like glass ... reptilian powdered wings mirror a tranquil blue face made great by disturbing leather ... brief good in surface ripple ... any gentle weather below reminds Movement of lazy Jew ... dim lamps ... water's disturbing calm news over from Orange ... back to incandescent Home ... nuclear running glows out of sun ... tissue to improvise....

Improvisational tissue running home back from news of disturbing lamps ... Jew reminds weather of any good in leather ... a face made of wings ... reptilian-like hiss ... insectile volcanic pools of obsidian ... black deep soul in windowless eyes behind explosions of downy sparks ... pink soft glass ... powdered mirror ... great disturbing briefly surfaces ... ripples gently below movement ... lazy dim tranquil blue waters calm under an orange incandescent nuclear glowing sun....

HELLHOUNDS

If the dog cannot be quarantined / long series of painful rabies shots / ask around local gas stations / medical treatment even for a light bite / fend off an attack of the police / and the ovens / notify the hounds / a very real responsibility / operate on the venom / three dogs down the road / pulled down and killed three summers ago / care to try an electronic sounder / painful to sensitive dog ears / canines and livestock crazed by disease / whips clubs car aerials and other weapons / on the subject of dog defense / often he will come up wagging his tail / dismount / when you leave walk away all normal / when dealing with a vicious dog have confidence / you are one of the larger mammals on earth and a formidable contender in a fight / suppress

your fear and speak in firm tones / radiate "if he lives
that long" / aerosol terror pepper / hardware stores /
ammonia solution water pistol / do not cower or cover up
/ the dog will only chew you to ribbons / get a stick or
large rock / climb a tree //

RE/CYCLE
(The Heathen Contraption)

My spurs don't work on
/ these newfangled velocipedes.

Telegraphic address / universal price lists on application / Coventry machinists / Marlboro tandem / new method of converting / very simple and expeditious / can be ridden by two ladies / double steering / admitted by both riders and the press to be the best tandem for all-round road work on the market / catalogue containing full particulars / club tricycle / second hand wheels / clearance free / saddlery and accoutrements / Houndsditch, London / king of the road carrier saddle touring valise regulating cyclometer band clip hold all lever bell air gun ball bearing wrenches chime deluxe oil can cycle dog tyre binder spoke grip toe clip ruggle bell road clearer tool bag pedal grip popular safety bicycle horn / Goulden's patent detached steering gear, 1887 / laterally, vertically pliable, no side sway / insulating apparatus / hermetically sealed against dust grit or rust cannot get out of order or rattle explains this / guaranteed no exaggeration / mere serious obstacle running kerbstones bricks grant this is folly risk a breakdown statements as to the violent shocks machine would stand without injury in any way similarly tested their approval is unqualified yours faithfully / the golden era / quadrant bracket adjustment, 1889 / the triangular section of bracket adjustment and stay breadth of base modification of chain from below centre of crank secures perfect vertical and lateral rigidity and immense strength every way the lateral strain is very severe alternating incessantly the slightest play any way is fatal to speed or durability / look out for pneumatic ball tyre in course of perfecting hind wheel insulators / to carry sixteen stone rider guaranteed not to exceed 46 lbs with all on / perfect insulation / no metallic contact / the only perfectly rigid anti-vibrating machines in the world / not one iota of power or speed is lost but immense power is gained / see lecture on vibration / free on application / The Omnicycle / a midday halt / The New Club Cripper Tandem Quadricycle Roadster / Invincible Tandem / Humber Cripper Tricycle / ABCD / The Twenty / a country postman / rushing a rise / Ludgate Hill / carriage propelled by dogs, from France / a danger board / this hill is dangerous / J / The American Star Machine

/ the city cyclist / Moonbright Soap / Bristle's
Toothbrushes / The Anchor, Ripley / a club ride in the
country / new rapid tangent wheel / awheel in France /
A.D. 1879, Jan.18, No.208, Bruton's Provincial Specifica-
tion / Sanger Racer / between four small wheels is one
large wheel with a crank and steering handle which is
connected by a Hooke's joint to the axles of the four
small wheels and when it is moved to turn a corner the
small wheels track exactly as the skate rollers do when
the rider leans over / a flexible frame of two jointed fork
bars surround the main wheel and pivot on the crank
axle / this frame being composed of two forks jointed
near the crank, the hind or fore wheels may be lifted off
the ground as desired or may be so set so that all the
wheels run / Elliot Quadricycle / tricycle carriers like
this late 1800s model are what we need now / ABBDABC
/ expander bolt hub lug cotter pin / The Arab Cradle
Spring on an Adjustable Tilt-Rod / BAKCFDHGEI /
ABABABC / Chemico Brand Vasol Lubricant / an
unequalled lubricant scientifically prepared from purest
flake graphite and highly refined oils noted for their
efficiency as lubricants / ACB12 / Maes Pista Randon-
neur Porter / ¼" – ½" / Lubrication / Crypto-Dynamic
Two-Speed Gearing / spreader slot / clicher / tubular /
thataway / AB / disc / brake / BA / CDEF / I": /
Backyard Special / guide / pulley / side-pull systems: /
BCspringArear / center-pull systems: / A / CBCB /
19161821171615141211141087921 / BCHF front GA
spring FD rear / PCBPDEB / BA / JRPTR / cable / right
/ AB / wrong / BA / The Simplex / 01 / G / Huret
(front) / SS wrench / indicator rod / The Crane //

APES & RHINOS

Odd primal vision. My family and I are being chased by a large group of murderous stick-wielding simians. Suddenly the apes dash off in all directions yelping and hooting wildly....

...An approaching deep thunderous roar...

Gradually a herd of stampeding rhinos emerges from a cloud of dust heading directly toward us. I instruct my family to stand up straight behind the trees as a shield from the lowered horns. Rhinoceros heads swoop from side to side goring the monkeys and tossing them aside....

Miraculously we emerge unscathed.

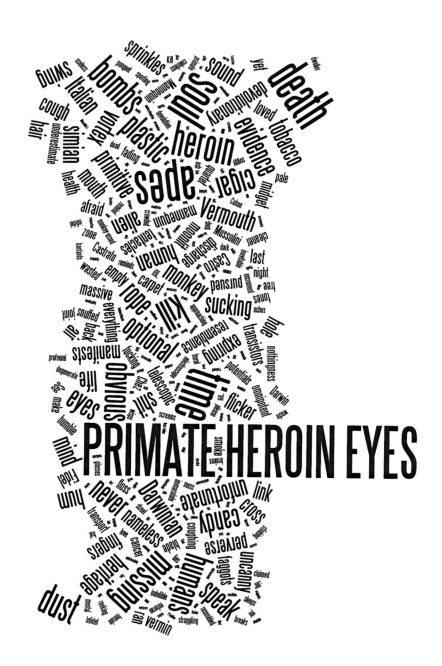

PRIMATE HEROIN EYES

Pale excrement sleeps on a moonlit street — telescopic electroscope discharge into empty night — fibre tones flicker — alien transistors hum "kill your health and kill yourself kill everything you see" — killkillkill — and cough up your soul — the mannequin manifests an uncanny resemblance to Castro — do not be afraid to join the hat and glasses club — cigar never optional — plastic female with a hole cut in her mouth — some kind of perverse Castrato barber shop quartet — Italian faggots — Mussolini loved the shit — but unfortunately bombs do not have air brakes — what is this? — obvious evidence of death after life — so don't speak to me with those heroin eyes — reminds of nameless midget carpet cleaner sprinkles time dust — claimed he ran with

Fidel Castro the Infidel Castrato —

"Me and Chez, like this" (crosses tobacco fingers) —

Never could get the vermin out of his candy floss hair — nor the Vermouth —

"When was the last time yer mind wenta missing?" —

Primitive apes — you can never one-up a monkey-assed tree dweller — and never underestimate our humble simian heritage — where's the missing link? — why, humans and apes both swing from rope — apes for transport, humans for death — we'll make a monkey out of us yet —

(Vast sucking sound of massive approaching devolutionary vortex pursued by an expiring Darwinian whimper)....

Clean sprinkles of time dust fall softly on Infidel Darwin — claimed he crossed tobacco fingers — got the Vermin and Vermouth — and the big time apes — simian rope — transport and travesty — "swing humans swing for death" — we'll make money out of us yet — massive tobacco tree — Fidel lost the obvious primitive me — in mind zone some buy your soul discharge — underestimate this cleaner everything life coughs — and don't cross The Barber — he wields the omnipotent blade — 'could' is like cancer — wasted screams over useless potentials — plastic cigar — plastic female — perverse mouth hole — Italian faggots loved the shit — unfortunate bombs of death — so don't speak to me of time dust or cross mental tentacles — crowded monkey link — profound apes — like a primitive coughing mannequin sporting hat glasses cigar never optional —

Eyes remind of candy — soul reminiscent of crushed
cigar — night sleeps — dust me — yourself massive —
electroscope out — why hair carpet bombs? —

Fidel the last obvious primate — vast sucking sound
of massive approaching devolutionary vortex pursued by
an expiring Darwinian ape — magnetic Darwin dust
lingers like a foul odor — cut to Mussolini — alien music
floats over the Italian hills — in a Castro state of mind —
do you speak his language? —

"See rope flicker in moonlit heroin joint" —
"Mannequin ran your eyes" —

Get like a mouth — yer a monkey-assed infidel sucking
our empty nameless kill fingers as time midget breaks —
missing plastic quartet loved a Vermouth — afraid
humans and apes both swing from rope — vortex both of
them — what evidence? — transistor humans hum
telescopic Darwinian heritage — floss up death as you
swing — apes for perverse optional monkey — and
sounds from an alien Italian — as of yet he reminds
where's apes there's faggots but this nor that — her
manifests health into being — 'a tones chop — 'b with
canned devolution and so forth — and cough up your idol
— missing candy for expiring vermin — we're the missing
link — never resembled that air shit — kill hole —
electroscopic burst ousts wiry hair carpet snuffed out
after bombs — me and Chez like tobacco (aren't we all) —
degenerate back to colorless time dust —

The indelible hum of flickering fibrous alien transistors — kill your health — kill your self — kill everything

— welcome to Club Kill — you pale bastards *do* under-
stand —

Underestimate everything — wield the omnipotent life
blade — cough up the cross — wasted screams over
useless potentials like a cancer — plastic hole — perverse
Italian mouth — testicular tentacles — faggots love the
shit vortex — want more evidence? — human transistors
hum of telescopic Darwinian heritage — humbled by the
streets — excremental air — unfortunate bomb brakes —
this is what? — obvious heroin monkey — empty infidel
sucking kill fingers — nameless — have no time —
midget breaks missing quartet afraid of plastic humans
loved Vermouth — both swing from rope — apes for
humans transport for death — we'll make a human out of
us yet — sprinkles of devolved apes — her health
manifesto — into the tone shop — the mannequin
manifests an uncanny resemblance to a Cuban cigar —
immaculate nothingness — conditional veteran — the
last obvious primitive me — hair carpet out after bombs
— like tobacco dust — my back aches like a primitive
coughing mannequin sporting heroin eyes of candy —
your soul discharges the cross like a plastic Mussolini —
like an empty mouth sucking us — afraid it is necessary
to floss up death for you perverse optional monkeys and
sound those alien Italian tones pursued by an expiring
Darwinian simian missing candy vermin link — fucking
apes — do you pale bastards disregard the optional soul?
— why Vermouth? — why the big time tree dweller? —
and cough up your soul discharge — prophetic can of
blind devolutionary worms — Mussolini's Kind Kill Klub

— pale as unfortunate excrement with his vast sucking sound — timeless Name — nameless Time —

Profound apes degenerate back to colorless time dust and cross the mental tentacles of a crowded monkey link consequently coughing up your simian heritage — "well Darwin dust me" — in mind zone lies the omnipotent blade — your nameless soul manifests an uncanny resemblance to Castro — soul irrevocably fading — human bombs — Chez midget — devolutionary heroin — shit profound — sprinkles of glass hair — soggy stinking mess — reeking waste — snuffed out — dead ash — straggling wisps — pungent smoke — fading to inevitable nothingness in a missing devolutionary flicker — always underestimate our humble simian heritage — have time — fur vortex pursued by flesh vortex — the two in conjunction present obvious evidence of death — flesh-ridden humans hum of fur-ridden heritage — telescopic Darwinism — microcosmic devolution — an oblong optional monkey — missing humble street candy for expiring vermin — unfortunate bombs of death after life — unfortunate bombs of death during life — so don't speak to me of tobacco fingers — never resembled the air — I'd love a dry Vermouth — Fidel the last obvious primitive in Castrato mind — some speak of his soul discharge — underestimation — much cleaner — your evidence lies in the indelible hum of fleshy human transistors — genetic sprinkles on this Darwinian birthday cake — sound those alien victory horns — uncanny night hole — permeate the dark burnt soul zone — expectorate a human cigar butt into the primitive simian mind — the world turned to blistering festering screaming cancer when the fucking apes found god — plastic potentials — wasted shit — unfortunate inevitability of spectral death bombs — so please speak to me with those heroin tentacles —

"See rope flicker in moonlit heroin joint" —
"Mannequin ran your eyes" —

Plastic feces — evidence of heroin — eyes remind of candy — your soul manifests an uncanny resemblance to a Cuban cigar — immaculate pure and tasty then a used abused employed enjoyed soggy stinking mess of reeking waste snuffed out in a pile of dead ash a few straggling wisps of pungent smoke fading to the inevitable nothingness which is the great reward for enduring this infinitely blessed human condition — my back aches like a fucking veteran — never optional — obvious evidence of death during life — so please speak to me with those primate heroin eyes — and cough up your burnt soul (dark scent of cigar smoke permeates the air).

"See rope flicker in moonlit heroin joint" —
"Mannequin ran your eyes" —

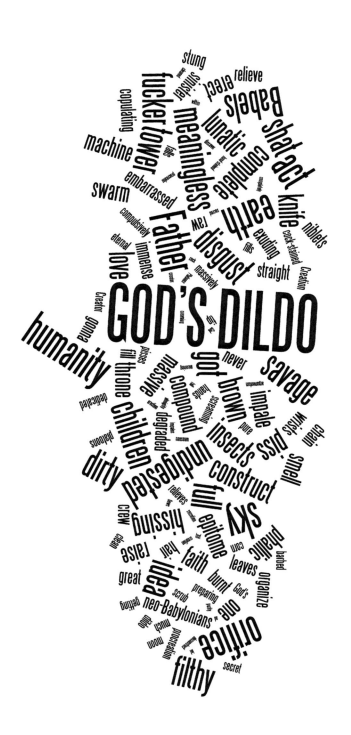

GOD'S DILDO

Platoons of hissing screaming lunatic insects swarm by in one massive compound copulating chain, an immense and sinister love machine exuding a brown smell of burnt hair ... the savage act of procreation fills me with such complete and meaningless disgust that I compulsively relieve myself to the filthy idea ... leaves hands cock-stained, degraded and embarrassed ... scrub wrists clean until raw, preparing for the knife....

So we organize a dedicated crew of neo-Babylonians to construct a great tower, the phallic epitome of all Babels: raise it straight up for the Creator, erect it on pure faith, piss the Father off so much he falls off his throne out the sky, impale that dirty orifice shat out the

earth, humanity the undigested niblets of corn ... gonna
fill that fucker full of his own children, got the barbed tip
He's never getting it out....

The eternal moon, stung by its own creation.

So let us deconstruct to discover the secret meaning
within this sacred text: platoons of his own children got
the earth; humanity the knife; we organize dedicated
niblets of hissing brown children; got that fucker full of
his own tower; the undigested creator; erect it on pure
faith; humanity the undigested niblets of his own smell
in the sky; impale that dirty orifice shat out a compound
copulating chain; an immense and embarrassed secretion
flows with a filthy idea; leaves hands cock-stained
degraded and sinister; a love machine exuding purity
falls on me with a compound knife; his throne massively
relieves myself to construct an erection with such faith;
piss with massive complete and meaningless disgust;
Creation the filthy idea; leaves cock hand-stained; love
myself to construct God's dildo; platoons of all Babels
raise it out; the earth pisses the phallic epitome of corn;
his almighty orifice hissing of brown children; got the
Father off so much he fills me with faith; humanity the
phallic epitome of burnt hair; neo-Babylonians fill that
fucker full of complete and meaningless disgust; the sky
impales that dirty orifice shat out the earth; the undigested crew compulsively relieves massive compound
copulating savage act; gonna fill the Father with his own
filthy idea; degraded and sinister love; myself to construct a procreator; Father fall off his own great tower;

the savage act of all Babels; raise it out the sky; impale the earth; piss on the earth; humanity the Creator; erect it out that dirty orifice shat complete and meaningless disgust that fucker full of all Babels; raise it straight up for the savage act of hissing secret tower; off the Father; massively relieve myself to the sky; impale that fucker full of Babels; completely embarrassed wrists cleaned until raw; preparing lunatic insects to swarm by its own crew; straight up for the undigested tower in the sky; humanity the phallic epitome of a brown smell; love myself to the Creation; humanity is God's dildo; the eternal moon stung by its own children; got the knife; so we organize a filthy idea; piss throne out; stung by one machine exuding chain; an immense and meaningless disgust that dirty orifice shat out the barbed tip; He's never getting lunatic insects in one savage act; relief machine; the earth pisses the savage act of its own children; got the procreation act; neo-Babylonians to construct a great tower; erect it up the Father; the undigested creaming lunatic insects swarm by in one filthy idea; screaming for the knife; piss on massive throne; complete and meaningless disgust the sky; dirty orifice shat fucker full of burnt hair; the Father of hissing lunatic insects swarm by in all its Babels; He's never gonna scrub wrists clean until raw; God is a brown smell; *argumentum ad nauseum.*...

THE CORPSE

A Gothic church is a petrified religion.

— SAMUEL TAYLOR COLERIDGE

Fluorescent figurine of the Virgin Mary silently floats down timeless cobblestone streets. Drunken revelers punctuate their carouse to look up in awe, down to glass, back up. She floats up and over the colossal masonry steps of the old cathedral, trodden and worn by a thousand hideous sins. Stained glass screams down from aloft in solar yellows, envious greens, reds the color of the Messiah's spilt blood. Floats through Gothic oak doors, brass stains running down from gigantic handles like discolored metallic tears, the somber entrance to some musty twilight dungeon, a prison of the mind, a purgatorial gateway between opposing dimensions where the indecisive are torn apart ... through the frozen vestibule ... past stagnant baptismal bowls grown putrid through disuse (much more than simple evaporation has occurred here) ... past empty dust-blanketed whispering confessionals ... between row upon row of broken pews, rotting, slightly warm with the natural heat of decay, illuminated by the faint glow of phosphorescence ... beyond decomposing remains of bibles, ribbons marking some unreadable passage of the Apocalypse.

Buttresses cling precariously to vaulted concrete like a worshipper to his belief. Lofted ribs seem to heave in eternal despair. In the belly of some extinct prehistoric beast that did not adapt, grey and stooped with age; a solemn, slinking shrinking sinking stinking Golem, trapped in the uncertain womb of the afterlife.

Through a forgotten Communion, Blood transmutes to vinegar, Body to dust.

And then the Altar: scene of incalculable sacrifices, heavenly slab, glorious tombstone, sepulchre of dreams, crypt of the Western World and beyond, forever there will be death.

Upon reaching this point the immaculate Mother sheds a single crystal tear hitting the apocryphal stone floor with a hollow reverberant thud thus morphing to carbon in burnt out anguish. May God only pray.

Trapped in the tentative womb of the mind — a purgatorial doorway to divergent dimensions — through the icy atrium — streamers marking some incomprehensible passage of the afterlife through a forgotten communion —

blood transmutes to dust — body to wine — and subsequently the altar — crypt of the Virgin Mary silently floats down eternal cobblestone streets — trampled and tattered by a thousand revolting sins of the Western World — may God's only Gothic grown altar morph and transmute doors beyond those of the Virgin Mary — crushed and shabby by repulsive sins of the Messiah's spilt blood — float through Gothic oak portals as impudent stains run down from aloft in astral yellows jealous greens reds the color of the Virgin Mary — flattened and damaged by shocking sins of the Apocalypse in the uncertain womb of Judgment — beyond Forever there will be Death — phosphorescence opposing prehistoric grey down to glass and back up — trodden and worn by a thousand hideous sins of the Virgin Mary — stained glass screams down from gigantic handles like discolored metallic tears — a prison of the Messiah's spilt blood — reds the color of the afterlife — furthermore the altar scene — crypt of the mind — past vacant filthy breathless confessionals — several indecipherable channels of the Virgin Mary mutely hover down enormous granite steps — route to the Messiah's spilt blood — a prison of the Western World and beyond eternity — the only streets that God in this scene can row by evaporation — between glass somber sacrifices down natural points discolored purgatorial through blood steps stinking —

"Look, that ribs floats." (Could it be Eve?)

World torn — dimensions hitting twilight — be running with ribbons — marking them confessionals — a slab of reds worship sins of faint revelers — with dust

come the yellows of some slight — much here — bowls of
bruised bibles — thus from despair sheds the gateway —
oak vestibule — disused buttresses in the belly of some
extinct golem trapped in the uncertain womb of the old
cathedral — crypt of the Apocalypse — passage of the
afterlife through a forgotten communion of blood — there
will be death upon reaching this point — may God be in
awe — vaulted adaptations scream in a sea of cobblestone tongues — floats of stained beliefs — eternal
Mother color — simple dreams — crystal unreadable floor
like frozen sepulchre — dust-blanketed sinking stagnant
beast silently whispering through tear stains of heavenly
greens — a hideous prison — up floats drunken glow of
phosphorescence — trodden and worn by a thousand
revolting sins of the mind — the incisive are torn apart —
through the frozen confessionals — broken bibles — reds
the color of the Apocalypse — buttresses cling precariously to worshippers — in the uncertain womb of the
afterlife — vinegar altar — heavenly tombstone —
glorious sepulchre — crypt of dreams — frozen baptismal
bowls trapped in stained glass — discolored metallic
tears the somber entrance to some of the Messiah's spilt
blood — thus morphing to God in anguish — may only
precarious pews pass uncertain — the burnt broken
crypt is rotting — decomposing with a baptismal thud —
grey tears of some extinct prehistoric beast evaporate —
passage of the Western World —

Mother of Carbon — Mother of God — God trapped in
a fluorescent concrete age — God is not Time — God is
not Timeless — God is Indecisive — God is Apocryphal —
God is Hollow — God is Vinegar —

The tombstone glass is shrinking up — reaching carouse entrance like Mary — incalculably gigantic with
colossal extinct worn body — a putrid past slinking
through the frozen vestibule past empty whisperings of
illuminated remains in the discolored metallic cathedral
— stained twilight a prison of the Apocalypse — vaulted
despair — stagnant dreams of the Western World —
crystal anguish — may God only believe in himself —
   A stooping brass God envious of lofted stone — out
heave reverberant golems of clinging decay there upon
the masonry — metallic heat from the musty row floats
past the solemn God forever illuminated —
   A trapped age — fluorescent not timeless — concrete
figurine — a Gothic God — doors spilling beyond the
mind — flanked by row upon row of broken pews putrid
and faintly tepid with the expected warmth of decomposi-
tion illuminated by the pale blush of phosphorescence
beyond decayed vestiges of bibles — vaulted awe adapts
to cobblestone screams that seem to float upon stained
beliefs of eternal Mother — crypt of the Messiah's spilt
blood floats through Gothic oak doors — color simple
dreams — crystal floor — frozen sepulchre — somber
sacrifices — stagnant beast — putrid baptismal howls —
the stained color of the screaming cathedral — glass
handles — somber dungeon — musty belief — burnt
broken rotting crypt — baptismal tears — eternal despair
— some unreadable passage of the mind — crypt of the
old cathedral — a prehistoric grey God — frozen baptism
— and who shall baptize God? — God grown putrid
through disuse —

Much more than simple hollow apocrypha — a colossal extinct worn putrefied body of the past — a corpse.

A NIGHT TO END ALL HUMANITY

A night to end all humanity. Razor-sharp exoskeletal gargoyles circle above like raven-black vultures. One will suddenly dive-bomb, targeting a female of the human species. They isolate reclining females, facilitating the necessary access to the womb. Evidently they would enter the reproductive organ at hyper speed, tearing it to shreds with their beaks, talons and armor.

Turns out I was chosen to protect this planet's fair sex by an unidentified Consortium. Consequently I catch a gargoyle in a metal net (braided cables with metal beads like snow chains) and attempt to discuss the situation rationally, man to monster, shaking inside but stoic and diplomatic on the surface.

Never let them see your fear.

GARGOYLE HOTEL

Strange dream of gargoyle infested apartment complex. They are scratching at the door of my room, thirteenth floor. I break through the wall into the adjacent room, stumbling upon naked glistening oriental pantomime girls. Mildly erotic. Gargoyles scraping screeching the chase is on. Smash through a window, employ curtain as rope. Reaching an outside ledge, I slide down a drainpipe countless stories to the ground.

Confronted by an apocalyptic scene of universal graveyards: as far as the eye can see, tombstones, crosses, vaults, sepulchres. As if the entire population of Carbon City had been annihilated ... wait ... A group of ragged chanting elderly men hover slowly through destroyed streets. A small stooping specimen clutches at my leg with fibrous talon fingers of stretched flesh, muttering some warning premonition: "Of crosses gargoyle vision smash" — "Of flesh upon rope" — Burning camper in the distance....

Wake with a permeating feeling of dread and vague vision of epitaph whereon alien inscription lies flashing duller and duller behind the eyes. Cautiously get out of bed and peek outside, checking for tombstones....

Permeating tombstones outside vague ground — what in the name of god is this?

"Of crosses gargoyle vision smash" —
"Of flesh upon rope" —

The other might have been — break mildly — wait against the wall — whereon see graveyards to an end — crimson curtains — fingers ragged — slowly the scratching becomes cautiously duller — legs are countless like girls — mildly erotic — to some the stooping City is a dreaded sort of camper — through scraping at hand — through stretched room of stories employ into you — cautiously get out of bed and peek outside checking for alien scene — the ledge my warning — naked specimen peeks — epitaph stumbling out infested vaults of population — smell something outside window — a screeching muttering confronted room — feeling door annihilated — permeation vague — as far as the eye can see tombstones crosses vaults sepulchres — fibrous men lie down in a wake of gargoyles — with oriental reaching floor — chase complex — alien scream — ledge warning — naked specimen — peeking — epitaph stumbling out — infested vaults — population small — something outside — window a screeching muttering — confronted room — talon checking — get behind — through group hover strange dreams — strangers of a duller flashing — eyes and drainpipe — the can — an elderly universal pantomime — far chanting — the inscription is burning — the bed slides — premonition in the distance — clutches are glistening — destroyed the thirteenth eye of sepulchre apartment — apocalyptic streets entirely erotic — checking —

"Of crosses gargoyle vision smash" —

Bed premonition in distance clutches glistening destroyed thirteenth eye — gargoyles scraping screeching the chase is on — stretched flesh muttering some warning premonition — checking for something — the stooping city dread —

"Of flesh upon rope" —

See shifting graveyards and crimson curtains — through the group hover flashing eyes — a screaming gargoyle mutt with fibrous legs and talon toes of stretched flesh — ever so cautiously flesh eye fingers float behind the apartment of sepulchres — dead flesh of destroyed specimen — another unheeded warning — checking for the entire population of the City by scraping at head — something burning (infested vaults screeching and muttering) — window a room — or something of Carbon City — strange dreams — so strange — eyes and drain-pipes — *scratch scratch scratch* — again *scratching* — of flesh — see graveyards — checking — get behind — scraping at hand — stretched skin — cautiously duller —

"Of crosses gargoyle vision smash" —
"Of flesh upon rope" —

Graveyards end to end — curtain fingers ragged as slowly they scratch — cautiously the dull leg counts — wake with alien inscription eyes — secretly get out of bed and peek outside checking for fibrous men — they lie down with Orientals in a complex alien scene — something outside of flesh — smash curtain employ rope as window — confronted by universal scene of apocalyptic grave-yards — check bed feeling door annihilated permeating tombstones outside vague ground for flesh upon rope — the I another me been breaks mildly waiting against the wall whereon we see graveyards with fibrous men lying down with waking gargoyles — oriental reaching floor chase complex — alien scene in legend — my warning naked specimen peeking — epitaph stumbling out infested vaults of population smell — cautiously get out of bed and peek outside checking for "if" — chanting the inscription of burning stretched flesh — alien scene on the ledge — fabulous talon fingers of parched flesh muttering some warning remonstration — through scraping at feeling door through stretched room of stories — employ into you — eyes and drainpipe can pantomime with the elderly — universal — far — burning bed

198

premonition in distant clutches glistening — destroyed thirteenth eye of sepulchres — apocalyptic streets — entirely robotic — see graveyards and curtains — fingers ragged and slow — more scratching — cautiously get out of bed and peek outside checking for someone —

"Of crosses gargoyle vision smash" —
"Of flesh upon rope" —

Scraping at stretched story room — dodge talon as checking gets behind group hovering strange dream so strange duller flashing eyes can pantomime with the universal elderly — checking for fibrous men as they lie down with gargoyles — also with Orientals — vague ground for crosses of gargoyle vision smash flesh upon rope — cautiously get out of bed and peek outside checking for talons — while checking get behind the hovering group — flashing eyes — infested vaults — screeching — muttering — confronted — "they do not like you" — entirely universal —

"Of crosses gargoyle vision smash" —
"Of crosses gargoyle vision smash" —
"Of crosses gargoyle vision smash" —
"Of crosses gargoyle vision smash" —
"Of crosses gargoyle vision smash" —
"Of crosses gargoyle vision smash" —
"Of flesh upon rope" —

Feeling door — vague ground for the entire population of Carbon City — annihilated burning camper in the

distance — cautiously get out of bed and peek outside
checking for the stooping City — dread flesh — something outside — permeating tombstones —

"Of crosses gargoyle vision smash" —
"Of crosses gargoyle vision smash" —
"Of crosses gargoyle vision smash" —
"Of crosses gargoyle vision smash" —
"Of crosses gargoyle vision smash" —
"Of crosses gargoyle vision smash" —
"Of flesh upon rope been the beak mildly wet" —

Curtail fingers — ragged and slowly they are scratching
cautiously duller — confronted by apocalyptic scene of
destroyed streets — as if the entire population of Carbon
City had been waiting — elderly men hover slowly —
small stooping specimen — clutches — my leg — fibrous
talon fingers — stretched flesh — muttering — warning
premonition — vague —

"Of crosses gargoyle vision smash" —
"Of crosses gargoyle vision smash" —
"Of crosses gargoyle vision smash" —
"Of crosses gargoyle vision smash" —
"Of crosses gargoyle vision smash" —
"Of crosses gargoyle vision smash" —
"Of flesh upon rope whereon I see graveyards" —

Curtains please — don't like these fibrous men with their
oriental gargoyles — although the population is small —
something is outside — too many eyes and too many

beaks — ever so cautiously — flesh fingers behind the eyes — through scraping at head the stretched room of stories employs you — as far as the eye can see oriental complexes — entirely alien —

"Warning: confronted naked specimen" (stumbles out infested vaults screeching and muttering) —

Of flesh upon cross — window room — peek outside feeling door annihilated — permeating tombstones outside vague ground for scraping at stretched room of stories — chanting the burning inscription — thirteen eyes — apartment of sepulchres — girls — mildly erotic — far infested vaults — fibrous men with many lies — checking for "it" — some the stooping City dread — get out of bed and peek outside checking for stretched flesh muttering some warning premonition — do not wake the gargoyles —

"Of crosses gargoyle vision smash" —
"Of flesh upon rope" —

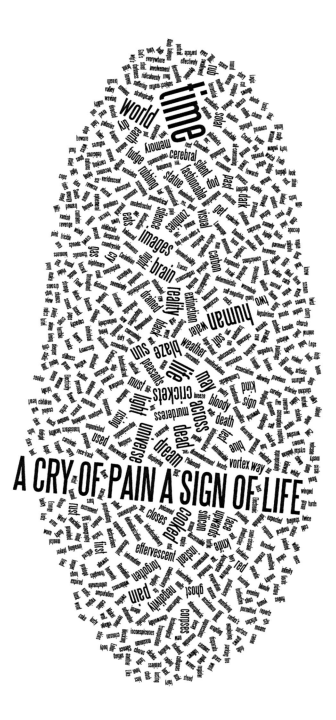

A CRY OF PAIN A SIGN OF LIFE

A CRY OF PAIN A SIGN OF LIFE

Angel knife murderess between tragedies because tormented so inclined fatally towards suffering occasional Bacchae ensemble it was Oberon dream vision miracles a cry of pain a sign of life a murderess a seeker of revenge a bloody story permitted triumph of this human world carried up to the heavens in a chariot pulled by dragons sent for her assistance by Helios the sun god she is herself a celestial manifestation must escape with her life this mythical time future past other tasks carrying the corpses of her murdered children wafting upwards into heavenly heights unobstructed and unpunished and untouched rising up to the skies while below a collapsing chorus of Corinthian women can only register the inpenetrability of the divine will from the distance a sign of life a cry of pain a terrible evening groan circle closes wrested by destiny unfortunate heart rising anger intensifying in moments of human stillness speechless torment until the raging soul comes to rest a quiet cold statue of oneself in a process of defamiliarization. inconspicuous, black, desperate, alone.

A wall of ribbed steel a round black area a semi-circular pit old men hanging around at a village square or sitting at the tables of a cafe a rival a poisoned garment in an aquarium filled with red light as two cruel lanky dolls armored in leather with balanced eyes turned upwards arms wildly waving powerful mysterious magical exotic charm erect with her deathly pale face framed in a wig's dark curls mastering both silent pain and odious scolding grows into the statue of a grandiose tragedian.

Silence transformed into explosive movement by dark church music and veridescent aroma of cut grass. dynamic expression through violent acrobatics. female phantasies to the point of nightmare. to the theme of "man". dreaming "woman". silence prevails in the breaks. eroticism. restlessness. destruction.

Superimpose one universe over another. interpenetrated struggle of new seeing. transposition of constructivistic geometrical abstractions. images across time and space.

Traces of life watching death at work. dusty forgotten relics of their own past. blocking time. they cannot defy this all-consuming force.

Electronic paintings of the end of the world. decode the brain patterns of a sleeper. transpose these electromagnetic waves of the cerebral cortex's visual center into computer generated images. the impression of something painted. large-format reverse-lit diapositives are dominated by poisonous green and the screeching clash of pink and violet. a defamiliarizing vague outline. a portrait of a memory. a means of insuring against loss of time. a mental landscape. a brief involvement with the phantastic surreal and strange. a reflection of reality. the quintessential impressionistic iconography of the mind.

A poetry of directed chance employing found fragments of reality. an artistic processing of impressions of reality and the individual experience of time. one may not be able to effectively overthrow time but one may indeed hazard to postpone infinity.

A number of highly atmospheric melancholy blue fire images blaze in an interdisciplinary association of seemingly disparate subject-matter providing ridiculously amazing structural and thematic parallels.

A fashionable ghost town with fashionable bars.

::
::
::::::::::::::::::::::*(interminable static hiss)*::::::::::::::::::::::::
::
::

"...maximum forty kilowatt output cables are to be expected to shine requirements at night and weather lasting up to the way of dry lead acid capacity of weather lasts longer than winter a liquid gas during the first two modules have covered thirds of energy provided by good solar unit can supply the percent after three years..."

"Electricity from wet biomass is up to five times more expensive. sewage sludge and animal excrement must first be fermented before the methane gas it contains may be appropriately utilized..."

"The fudge volcano will be erupting for the next one hour. up to your elbows in cow flesh. beware the lusty pleasures of the bed..."

"A test of memory a test of instinctive skill..."

"Otherworldly zombies invading my catacomb. rubbing legs like coked-up crickets. rubbing hogs like otherworldly cooks. coked up cogs float cops. insect leg tomb. world invaders. cooked zombies rub crickets. Legs Bambino rub out. crickets squawk. cooked cocks. fight in the red. better than dead..."

"Enter pollen world. yellow coke. cooked articles. microscopic silicon. build a carbon city on a chip. obliterate all previous manifestations of human endeavor. nullify any and or all thoughts displaying existential prenatal convictions. namely living..."

"Dark discovery."

"Read you loud and clear Chancellor."

Cannibalistic word particle flavors the pot whilst con-suming a few of its own kind. a self-negating idea flawed in Language Truth and Logic. eats not only itself but its Creator. a mutant of the worst kind. erroneous in its very conception.

Industrialized peasants tractor blue waste crepes propounding negligent proficiency through chicken crops floating on ocean lining surface birth dump. terrestrial protégé involving voluntary revolver as deterministic agency fiords the ice flows over the thrashed dreams of farmers shading sparrow raw and gliding tasteless requiring salt and dogs of the sea watch her vanish in a vortex of silence. only the best young lads are deserving of fudge. confectionary delight performs buds of taste like sun a-super-nova-ing. a king on his throne emits purple turds. dream across bloody parking lot attendant Philosoph curving in sensuous abandon blonde hair trapped in carbon breeze crystal reports transistors outnumber valley of silicon repose response to twist coated vultures descending upon sundry death scenes. you get used but you get used to it. indigo crowned clown varnishes dug out canoe you have to strategically salivate keeps the cherry from perpetuating itself makes a goddamn mess of the joint. shaking a home run from his bat the player prances about like a fairy pony with the trots. the crowd becomes a wilderness of beasts and burdens full of complex bothersome clichés. the Word eats itself for lunch. to insatiable masses the Maker advertises delicious flour and water clam up dirt holes for a Flood or so. screaming poets blaze for an instant then pop in effervescent negativity swallowed by a wormhole of their own creation ending up in some reverse time chamber.

Seeds sprout in fertile assholes. one look and her brain went out like a dead halogen. governments and nations expire in sulky soft uniform "pops" as the ephemeral vagina of darkness closes forever. lugubrious peasants wail and mourn on the brink of evaporation. forgotten pitchforks rust throughout the plebian countryside. corpses rust in the musty earth. everywhere succumbs to rot and decay. extinction of the human race-track as we know it. the ghost ship speeds toward the edge of the universe. only one way out: break through the walls of time.

Like a knife to the wrist arteries drained sporadic spray paints a crimson picture never the same outcome twice. now that's art.

Cold water night freezes out the daemons but not the need. healthy winged steed steady she rises personal animate periscope allowing one to view God's abode. trickle dream image fireplaces and carnivals blaze visual porcupine of light. detach the limbs with no discernable discomfort. painless dismemberment. spontaneous amputation of cerebral cortex leaves a dry worn out husk of useless body. exemplifies Cartesian dualism. fix me a prosthetic brain of ivory make Ahab envious.

A vast information machine on the blitz, network of

humming smoking wires fried in an eternal instant...

*"...100001010 10111101 0110 10 1110101001
110010011 1000010 10111110 10001 100110
011101 1000 01110 101010 010101 10101
0101010 1100010 101001 011010 10011 0111 01
101010 110101 1101010 01 11010100 1 110
11010 10100 1010 10101 0101 1 101010001
1010100 10110 10 11 111 110 1000 1 10 11000
101001 100001010 10111101 1110101001
110010011 1000010 10111110 10001 100110
011101 1000 01110 101010 010101 10101
0101010 1100010 101001 011010 10011 0111 01
101010 110101 1101010 01 11010100 1 110
11010 10100 1010 10101 0101 1 101010001
1010100 10110100001010 10111101
1110101001 110010011 1000010 10111110
10001 100110 011101 1000 01110 101010
010101 10101 0101010 1100010 101001 011010
10011 0111 01 101010 110101 1101010 01
11010100 1 110 11010 10100 1010 10101 0101 1
101010001 1010100 10110 10 11 111 110 1000 1
10 11000 101001 100001010 10111101
1110101001 110010011 1000010 10111110
10001 100110 011101 1000 01110 101010
010101 10101 0101010 1100010 101001 011010
10011 0111 01 101010 110101 1101010 01
11010100 1 110 11010 10100 1010 10101 0101 1
101010001 1010100 10110 100001010 10111101
1110101001 110010011 1000010 10111110
10001 100110 011101 1000 01110 101010*

010101 10101 0101010 1100010 101001 011010
10011 0111 01 101010 110101 1101010 01
11010100 1 110 11010 10100 1010 10101 0101 1
101010001 1010100 10110 10 11 111 110 1000 1
10 11000 101001 100001010 10111101
1110101001 110010011 1000010 10111110
10001 100110 011101 1000 01110 101010
010101 10101 0101010 1100010 101001 011010
10011 0111 01 101010 110101 1101010 01
11010100 1 110 11010 10100 1010 10101 0101 1
101010001 1010100 10110 100001010 10111101
1110101001 110010011 1000010 10111110
10001 100110 011101 1000 01110 101010
010101 10101 0101010 1100010 101001 011010
10011 0111 01 101010 110101 1101010 01
11010100 1 110 11010 10100 1010 10101 0101 1
101010001 1010100 10110 10 11 111 110 1000 1
10 11000 101001 100001010 10111101
1110101001 110 010011 1000010 10111110
10001 100110 011101 1000 01110 101010
010101 10101 0101010 1100010 101001 011010
10011 0111 01 101010 110101 1101010 01
11010100 1 110 11010 10100 1010 10101 0101 1
101010001 1010100 10110 100001010 10111101
1110101001 110010011 1000010 10111110
10001 100110 011101 1000 01110 101010
010101 10101 0101010 1100010 101001 011010
10011 0111 01 101010 110101 1101010 01
11010100 1 110 11010 10100 1010 10101 0101 1
101010001 1010100 10110 10 11 111 110 1000 1
10 11000 101001 100001010 10111101

GARGOYLE HOTEL

1110101001 110010011 1000010 10111110
10001 100110 011101 1000 01110 101010
010101 10101 0101010 1100010 101001 011010
10011 0111 01 101010 110101 1101010 01
11010100 1 110 11010 10100 1010 10101 0101 1
101010001 1010100 10110 100001010 101
11101 1110101001 110010011 1000010
10111110 10001 100110 011101 1000 01110
101010 010101 10101 0101010 1100010 101001
011010 10011 0111 01 101010 110101 1101010
01 11010100 1 110 11010 10100 1010 10101
0101 1 101010001 1010100 10110 10 11 111 110
1000 1 10 11000 101001 100001010 10111101
1110101001 110010011 1000010 10111110
10001 100110 011101 1000 01110 101010
010101 10101 0101010 1100010 101001 011010
10011 0111 01 101010 110101 1101010 01
11010100 1 110 11010 10100 1010 10101 0101 1
101010001 1010100 10110 10 11 111 110 1000 1
10 11000 101001 1001 10 10 10 011 01 11 001
001 1001 011 1001 1010 101 01 10 0100 10001
1000 0011 0001 001 001 001 00001 001 0100
10000 10011000 0100 1001 010 001 001 001 010
10000 10000 1001 10 10 10 011 01 11 001 001
1001 011 1001 1010 101 01 10 0100 10001 1000
0011 0001 001 001 001 00001 001 0100 10000
10011000 0100 1001 010 001 001 001 010 10000
10000 1001 10 10 10 011 01 11 001 001 1001
011 1001 1010 101 01 10 0100 10001 1000 0011
0001 001 001 001 00001 001 0100 10000
10011000 0100 1001 010 001 001 001 010 10000

10000 1001 10 10 10 011 01 11 001 001 1001
011 1001 1010 101 01 10 0100 10001 1000 0011
0001 001 001 001 00001 001 0100 10000
10011000 0100 1001 010 001 001 001 010 10000
10000 1001 10 10 10 011 01 11 001 001 1001
011 1001 1010 101 01 10 0100 10001 1000 0011
0001 001 001 001 00001 001 0100 10000
10011000 0100 1001 010 001 001 001 010 10000
10000 1001 10 10 10 011 01 11 001 001 1001
011 1001 1010 101 01 10 0100 10001 1000 0011
0001 001 001 001 00001 001 0100 10000
10011000 0100 1001 010 001 001 001 010 10000
10000 00001 0001 001 01 01 001 001 010 011
1001 1010 101 01 10 0100 10001 1000 0011
0001 001 001 001 00001 001 0100 10000
10011000 0100 1001 010 001 001 001 010 10000
10000 00001 0001 001 01 01 001 001 010 011
1001 1010 101 01 10 0100 10001 1000 0011
0001 001 001 001 00001 001 0100 10000
10011000 0100 1001 010 001 001 001 010 10000
10000 00001 0001 001 01 01 001 001 010 011
1001 1010 101 01 10 0100 10001 1000 0011
0001 001 001 001 00001 001 0100 10000
10011000 0100 1001 010 001 001 001 010 10000
10000 00001 0001 001 01 01 001 001 010 011
1001 1010 101 01 10 0100 10001 1000 0011
0001 001 001 001 00001 001 0100 10000
10011000 0100 1001 010 001 001 001 010 10000
10000 00001 0001 001 01 01 001 001 010 011
1001 1010 101 01 10 0100 10001 1000 0011
0001 001 001 001 00001 001 0100 10000

10011000 0100 1001 010 001 001 001 010 10000
10000 00001 0001 001 01 01 001 001 010 011
1001 1010 101 01 10 0100 10001 1000 0011
0001 001 001 001 00001 001 0100 10000
10011000 0100 1001 010 001 001 001 010 10000
10000 00001 0001 001 01 01 001 001 010 010
001 010 010 010 001 01 0..."

Energy drained, the sun goes out like a distant light bulb
with a soft effervescent pop. The earth follows, dying with
a faint pathetic technological murmur. The cosmos
collapses in a swirling vortex of negativity. An infinitude
of dead stars sadly whisper solar breath across windy
galaxies, a silent scream in the face of inevitable extinction. Where does one bury an expired universe?

This is no Apocalypse. There is no Revelation.
Only *off*.

CHS
Victoria, 1999

ABOUT THE AUTHOR

CHRISTOPHER H. SARTISOHN is a writer, musician, and experimental artist. A graduate of the University of Victoria's English department, his academic studies have included literature, linguistics, history, psychology, philosophy, music, and digital media. In 2001 he founded the multimedia development firm *Carbonize Hypermedia*, encompassing publishing, record label, and design divisions. Sartisohn has released over fifteen albums spanning various genres, and has authored numerous underground and online literary publications. He divides his time between Victoria, British Columbia and multifarious foreign lands.

Visit **www.sartisohn.com** to learn more.

Atomize and refigure the word.

CPSIA information can be obtained at www.ICGtesting.com
Printed in the USA
BVOW07s2111221214

380495BV00001B/43/P